The Return Home

A novel by

Elliott J. Anderson

Published by Clifton Hills Press, Valparaiso, Indiana

 For information, please contact us at:
Clifton Hills Press
386 Deer Ridge Road
Valparaiso, Indiana 46385

Edited by Warren Anderson

Layout by Tim May

Cover art by Gabrielle Gizzi

Printed in the United States of America

ISBN-13: 9780915725236

To Bill Porter and Tim Morehouse, my writing teachers at Seven Hills High School in Cincinnati, Ohio, two very different men who were equally influential in my academic development and in my maturation as a young man. Their patience, persistence, and inspiration went well beyond the classroom.

Contents

Chapter 1

The time for celebrating Christmas was officially over – not just for this year, but forever. How many disappointments is one man expected to suffer during the holiday season without losing his Christmas joy? Ryan Miller had just closed the biggest account of his career, a contract which would secure his company for the foreseeable future. It was a partnership with a Fortune 500 company that he'd pursued for over a year. It certainly eased the pressure of the upcoming board meeting in early January, but he lacked the adrenaline rush that normally accompanied his victories. He wanted to be happy – to celebrate – but he couldn't. His steely focus was blurry. His sharp analytical processing was dull. His obsessive attention to detail was missing. He was tired and didn't believe he'd been at his best the last two days, so he was actually shocked the agreement came to pass.

Ryan was CEO of Emerging Enterprises, a mergers and acquisitions company he'd taken to new heights in the last five years. The sign on his office door declared his status as he locked it for the night – as did the scrolling video he walked past in the empty foyer of the glass-walled entryway and the brick facade as he exited the building. "Emerging Enterprises," he said slowly and out loud as he glanced over his shoulder after setting the alarm. "Ryan Miller, CEO." It was one of the repetitious habits he did as he left every night to remember what was at stake and what his position required of him. Emerging was the only firm he'd ever known besides his family's business back home. He started at Emerging as an intern from Powell University. Hired the fall after his graduation, he worked his way up the corporate ladder and made all the necessary sacrifices along the way. And now, a week before Christmas, wealthy and alone, he walked the two blocks to the parking garage in stunned silence.

Chapter 1

He slid into his black Audi R8 and looked at the text again. "Honey, I know you won't pick up the phone," his mother wrote, "but your father finally died. Please come home for the funeral on Tuesday." He tossed the phone on the passenger seat without emotion and drove aggressively out of the garage and into the empty streets. His father had been in a coma for six months with little chance of recovery, so his death was not a surprise. Neither was the fact that Ryan was driving home after 9:00 p.m. He found it peaceful to leave the office late at night when the rest of the city was conveniently and comfortably at home. He actually preferred to work late when the employees who counted on him were gone, and he could focus on his own "to do" list without the constant demands. He loved being the CEO with the money, title, and status, but the role, despite its perks, left him with little time for anything else, and he was exhausted. In response to his fatigue – and for a sardonic outlet the last six months – Ryan had created a funny list of descriptions of what the acronym for CEO really meant. He made these up to make fun of himself and to take the edge off his own expectations. Ryan recorded them on his phone and even had a record of them on an Excel spreadsheet where he ranked them in order of preference. So far, Completely Exhausted Officer, Chiefly Economically Obsessed, and Calculated Emotionless Officer were his favorites and ranked at the top. Most of them came to him without much thought. He didn't know if that was a good sign or a bad one.

Ryan pulled into his four-car garage attached to his beautifully rehabbed Tudor mansion in the Wooded Pine subdivision and looked mindlessly at his other sports cars. He loved how they looked, but he wasn't even a car enthusiast, so besides rotating which car he drove each week and what color the cars were each year, he found little enjoyment in his toys. He entered the voice-activated sliding glass door back entrance and was met by the friendliest and most worthless guard dog in the subdivision. Buford greeted Ryan in the kitchen with his traditional circle dance, and Ryan kneeled down for hugs and kisses. Buford, a nine-year old middle-sized chocolate lab, still acted like a puppy, but he gave Ryan exactly what he needed every day: unconditional love, support, joy, and affection. Ryan threw his coat on the couch and his computer bag onto the chair and played rope tug with Buford, relaxing for the first time all day. "Christmas Eventually Over," Ryan said to Buford, and he laughed at his newest CEO title which now had morphed into contextual events while he glanced at the December 17th date on the calendar. It didn't totally fit the list criteria and wouldn't make the spreadsheet top 10, but today felt like a day for improvisation.

Ryan continued to communicate with Buford as he went through his nighttime routine. He found himself talking to Buford more and to people less, and he hoped this wasn't a mental health problem. He changed into his sweats and turned on the television, usually CNN or ESPN, mindless noise, really, because he never sat down to actually watch. It was simply for background company and the voices of humans who didn't need him. He grabbed his phone to request his late-night dinner. It was Friday, which meant Chinese food, and manager Li Wei, recognizing Ryan's number and the day of the week, finalized the order before either one bothered with an introduction. "I'll have it delivered in 20 minutes," Li Wei said curtly and hung up without waiting for Ryan's customary thank you. *Am I that predictable*, he wondered? He checked his mail and tossed most of it – unopened – into the recycling bin and then told Buford to get his leash. Buford complied with much enthusiasm, and Ryan wished his employees obeyed him as quickly. Man and his best friend walked into the night for their customary obligations. Ryan rhetorically asked Buford which direction he wanted to go, and Buford chose the way he chose every night. He headed toward the path in the woods that circled the perimeter of the south side of the subdivision. Ryan owned a triple lot with more land and woods than his neighbors. He liked the privacy and the nature. He took a deep breath of chilly, winter air and let Buford lead the way.

Ryan was still in denial about his father's death and had yet to respond to his mother's announcement. He also ignored a couple of voice mails from his little sister Jennifer. He would enjoy his walk with his dog and call his mom and sister tomorrow, but after work. He always worked Saturday mornings. Well, maybe that included Saturday afternoons also, but it rarely included his normal 12-hour weekday workday. Ryan loved his mother and sister, but they didn't really understand him or the complicated relationship he'd had with his father. Halfway through the walk he ignored yet another call from his mom, but he knew he needed to text her before she went to bed, or she would call him every hour and all night long. For her sake, and so she could sleep, he texted her that he would be home on Sunday, but he needed 24 hours to prepare his company and himself for his absence. Finally, he said he was really sad for her and knew his dad was a great husband. Ryan stared at his message for a couple of seconds before he sent it, soaking in the truth of the loss and why he couldn't mention his dad as a great father, as well. He turned off the phone and shoved it in the inner breast pocket of his coat. Buford wanted to pick up the pace, but that was the opposite of what Ryan needed – on this walk and in his life. Even though Emerging shut down the week between Christmas and New Year's, the week before Christmas was always hectic and chaotic and Ryan hated it. At least now he would miss this annual week of torture, including the office Christmas party where he had to pretend he loved the evening and big crowds. This thought actually warmed his heart in a strange and comforting way.

Chapter 1

Buford finished his walk, and the two cold and hungry friends approached the front of the house just in time to meet the delivery driver with Ryan's food. Ryan gave his favorite driver Jacob a $50 tip and a "Merry Christmas" and headed inside with Buford. They ate their meals in tandem as Buford also loved Orange Chicken. Ryan cleaned up their meals and then went to his coat and retrieved his phone. He turned it back on and saw his mom had texted him back: "OK, dear. I look forward to seeing you Sunday. Your father loved you." Ryan laid the phone on the counter and pulled out his laptop and checked his email. There was only one new one, so he read it quickly and deleted it. *Who sends emails at 10:30 p.m. anyway?* Ryan thought and then laughed at himself. *I guess I do.* He paused for a moment and stared at the family picture on the wall before breaking his evening routine. He split his screen from the email and pulled up his pictures file and a folder with some old family photos. There were some nice family memories of trips to California, Florida, Paris, and Rome and a few good portrait pictures of the four of them before the separation with his father occurred. But it was a picture of someone else that really grabbed his heart. In one of the family photos from a July 4th party at their family home a lovely, tall blonde was right next to Ryan. It was Heather.

Ryan had dated many women over the past ten years, but he hadn't been in a relationship with a woman since his early 20's. Heather Hayes was from his hometown, Sugar Grove, Minnesota, and worked for his father's candy company, the North Pole. She had also graduated from Powell but was two years younger than Ryan. She was in Jennifer's class and one of Jennifer's best friends. Ryan and Jennifer attended Sugar Grove Academy, the local private school founded by their grandparents, so they didn't know Jennifer until college. She had attended the local public Sugar Grove High School. Ryan met Heather the first time Jennifer brought Heather home for the weekend and the immediate chemistry was obvious, but they didn't start dating until Heather was in her internship at North Pole the summer between her sophomore and junior years. That was Ryan's last summer working at North Pole, and that season together initiated their two-year romance. Everyone expected them to get married and everybody expected Ryan's career to be at North Pole, but Ryan was independent and stubborn and wanted to carve his own path. This caused friction with Heather and, honestly, with everyone in his family.

According to the family plan, Ryan was supposed to take over North Pole when his father retired, working his way up the leadership command in the process, but Ryan refused every invitation, plea, and persuasion to follow those marching orders. The issue became contentious seven years ago when the COO left North Pole, creating the perfect time for Ryan to transition into the company, but Ryan had just taken the

COO role at Emerging and didn't want to leave. The discussion turned into an argument, then a yelling match, and the relationship with his father was never the same after that. The two men had barely talked since. Heather was also devastated with Ryan's decision and their long-distance relationship was strained until it ended.

That conclusion culminated, three weeks after the family fight, on Christmas Eve at the North Pole Christmas Celebration, during which the whole town seemed to spend the week on the company's grounds. In reality, both Ryan and Heather wanted to get married and had discussed it many times, but Heather wanted to live in Sugar Grove and work at North Pole, and Ryan wanted neither of those destinations. She wouldn't leave and couldn't believe Ryan wanted to live in the city and away from his family. He wouldn't make the same salary at North Pole, but he would still do really well financially, and he'd still be the COO of a company.

Ryan told her he had to forge his own career alone (and he emphasized *alone*) and wanted to run his own company. He knew when he said it that way it was a mistake. On their way to the ice skating circle, Heather told Ryan he had to choose. It was Sugar Grove and her, or it was Emerging, and it was over. Ryan didn't answer right away and processed her passionate ultimatum as they walked the last 50 feet to the rink. When they reached the skate circle, he sat down to lace up his skates. Heather was furious with his silence, received that as his answer, and kept walking. Frustrated and confused, Ryan simply watched her leave.

After 10 minutes Ryan realized she wasn't coming back and he ripped off his skates, threw them in his bag and left the celebration immediately. He sped home, shoved his clothes in his suitcase and left. He didn't even stay home for Christmas. He left his parents a note on the kitchen table and went back to his condo in the city. It was the first of six straight Christmases alone with no tree, no lights, no decorations, and only a few presents – the ones his family and employees gave him because they thought they needed to. He donated most of them to charity. He only returned home now a few times a year, staying a day or two at the most. His mother let him know updates about the company, his family, and, of course, Heather, even when Ryan didn't want to know about any of them. Heather eventually married a Sugar Grove fireman, Josh Thomas, and had a son named Henry, who had to be about four or five now. Unfortunately, Heather divorced Josh after he disappeared a year and a half ago. Heather was devastated by the separation and went through a rough season, and it was Ryan's parents who were Heather's oasis during the crisis. Heather's parents had died in a car accident when she was in college and she was an only child, so she was all alone with Henry. Ryan thought of reaching out to Heather many times but never did. He was pretty sure Heather hated him. Ryan stared at the photo of the happy couple for way longer than he intended. Then he shut his laptop dramatically. He assumed he would see Heather at the funeral and had no idea what he would feel – or what he would say. He stood up and told Buford it was time for bed, and the two males shuffled to their restful domains. Buford's bed was right next to Ryan's bed. They both curled up in their blankets and were asleep in minutes.

Chapter 2

Ryan worked all morning at Emerging and video-called his mom Becky from the office after lunch. She scolded him for working on a Saturday, and he admitted he would probably work until about dinner but would be home by early afternoon tomorrow. She was upbeat and positive, as always, even while planning the details of her own husband's funeral. Jennifer, her husband Gabe, and their two children were also there. Becky and Jennifer had obviously been grieving but were both very organized women, and death required details and decisions. Becky quickly and efficiently walked through the last matters of the arrangements with her two children. Lastly, Becky asked Ryan to organize the open house at North Pole. It would follow the service and allow the community to pay their respects. She had a list of roles to be filled for the open house and encouraged Ryan to reach out to some of the community so they could be engaged in the memorial. Ryan repeated the list of jobs out loud as he wrote them down on his legal pad. They broke the list into three groups, each of them taking the lead on finding the people needed. When he finished pronouncing the list to his mom and sister for verification of responsibilities, a woman's face suddenly popped in front of his mother's and said, "Hey, Ryan. I'll take the hostess role at the front door to greet everybody." It was Heather. She must have been there the whole time. Ryan was so startled he just stared at her with his mouth open while Heather flashed her magnetic smile.

"So sorry Jim is gone, Ryan. Look forward to seeing you soon," Heather said casually to break the awkward silence before disappearing. Ryan gave his mother a playful glare when he returned to the screen while Becky acted as if nothing strange or different had taken place. Ryan hung up a few minutes later because he couldn't concentrate hearing Jennifer and Heather laughing in the background. His mother obviously enjoyed the moment of his discomfort; she couldn't quit grinning during their remaining conversation. She always had thought Ryan and Heather were supposed to be together.

Ryan had planned on working many more hours at the office, but seeing Heather changed everything. He quickly created a long email full of instructions for the week, sent it to his executive assistant Tammy, and hurried out of the building. Tammy Malone was an invaluable colleague, friend, and office manager. Her excellence in task management and follow through allowed Ryan to be his best. He also paid her almost as much as he did his Vice Presidents, though only his VP of Finance knew that reality. She was worth every penny.

On the way home Ryan called one of the few friends he still kept in contact with from Sugar Grove, the small timber town in Northern Minnesota where his family had settled in the 1920's. His great grandfather immigrated to Minnesota from Scotland and worked in timber his whole career. Ryan's grandfather Joe was the first family businessman and could have built his candy company anywhere and name it anything, but he decided to build it in Sugar Grove and call it North Pole. Grandpa Joe was the original Christmas fanatic in the family. When he was older, he grew out his white beard and would dress like Santa for the month of December. The children in the community actually believed he was Santa and that's when the North Pole Christmas Celebration tradition was started.

Grandpa Joe was a wonderful man, and Ryan had loved him more than anybody else in the world. He had spent hours following Grandpa around the factory. Ryan's nickname those first couple of summers at North Pole was Elf because Ryan did anything Joe wanted him or needed him to do. Joe was an inspirational leader and brought out the best in his employees. Joe saw Ryan's leadership ability and let him manage important responsibilities, even when he was in high school. By the time Ryan interned at Emerging he was already a gifted manager with a ton of experience. He had a knack for efficiency and effectiveness in business and with money. He had neither, however, when it came to love. Everyone said it was fitting when Grandpa Joe died on Christmas day in 2000. Ryan thought it was the cruelest irony ever. It was the start of his disdain for the Christmas season.

Steve was surprised to hear from Ryan but, as always, made time for his quiet and introverted friend. "Hey, Ryan, what's up?"

"You heard my dad died, Steve," Ryan said, as a matter of fact. "I'm coming home to Sugar Grove tomorrow and hoped we could grab a cup of coffee together."

"Yes, of course I did," Steve replied quickly. "So sorry for your loss. I'll make time whenever it is best for you next week. Text me a few options after you know the family schedule."

"Will do," Ryan confirmed. "Talk to you soon." His conversations with Steve were never long, but they didn't have to be – and that's part of the reason Ryan liked him so much. No demands. No requirements. Catch up once in a while. And Steve was someone he could open up to a little bit without fear or judgment.

****

Jennifer, Heather, and Becky had a good laugh about Heather's surprising presence during their video call with Ryan.

"What was it like seeing him?" Jennifer asked.

"It was great," Heather said, "but I don't think Ryan was ready for it. He doesn't know I hang out with you guys all the time. He looked a little surprised."

Becky chimed in. "I think he was startled by your beauty and your smile, Heather." This statement was truer than Becky knew.

"Aw, thanks," replied Heather. "That wasn't enough to keep him here six years ago, so I am sure nothing has changed now."

"He's older now," Jennifer retorted, "and I don't think he is happy anymore. All he does is work, and he has no one to share his life with in the city."

"There have to be a million girls after him in the city," Heather said casually, in a gentle attempt to pry information from her best friend and Ryan's sister. They had remained best friends after college and even survived the painful break-up with Ryan. In fact, Jennifer was the one who secured Heather's job at North Pole where she had worked ever since.

"He's had many dates," Jennifer replied, "but you are the only woman he ever brought home to meet the family."

"That doesn't count," Heather laughed. "I already knew you and had been in your home tons of times." All three ladies smiled with the memories.

"Well, I don't think he has ever gotten over you," Jennifer shouted as she headed outside to round up her children.

"I am not sure I have ever gotten over him either," Heather whispered to Becky as she gave her a hug and a kiss. "I'll see you tomorrow."

"Alright, Honey," Becky replied, nodding affectionately. "Jim loved you and believed in you – and your role in the company. Are you sure you don't want to pursue the CEO role now that it is officially vacant?" In respect for Jim, the board had decided not to pursue his replacement for at least the first year of his coma. After that, they were going to open the position up for a national search and, though it wasn't announced yet, they planned to post it on January 5th.

"I don't think so, Becky. Henry starts first grade next year and I am not interested in working 60 hours a week while being a single mother," Heather stated directly. "Maybe if Josh hadn't left I would have considered it. My new role is all the work I need, and I really enjoy it anyway."

The two ladies gave each other one more hug, and Becky saw Heather out the front door and onto the porch. By the time Becky returned to the kitchen, shouts of "Grandma, we're hungry" awaited her.

****

Ryan packed his bag as soon as he arrived home even though he wasn't leaving until the morning. Buford was confused by this activity and began to whine. "Don't worry, boy, you are going with me," Ryan assured him.

Ryan couldn't get the picture of Heather's smiling face out of his mind. Seeing her brought up so many memories. Most were happy, but some ultimately brought back the sadness of the end of the relationship. He began to talk to Buford again as he walked around the house. "Why did I leave her? Why did I just let her walk away?" Buford wagged his tail even harder as Ryan gave him a pat on the head. "I know. I know. Stupid, right?"

"I chose a career over a woman I loved," Ryan said self-condemningly. "What kind of idiot am I?"

This time Buford barked in response.

"You didn't have to agree with me, boy," Ryan said sadly, giving Buford a knowing nod.

Ryan reached for the phone and called the local pizzeria. It was Saturday night, so manager Mario Luigi of Luigi's Pizzeria's this time recognized Ryan's number and confirmed his order with very little conversation. Ryan could, of course, order all the food online, but he loved the rhythm and efficiency of his quick calls for dinner. He had created a small community within his self-care rituals and the absence of a family. None of the local restaurant managers in town knew they were a part of his family, but he looked forward to the consistency of contact even if it was all one-sided. He made sure to give a year-end gift to each of them that made any annoyance quite worth the process.

"Maybe I do need a change," Ryan told Buford without looking at him this time.

Again Buford barked accordingly. "Are you trying to tell me something, buddy?" Ryan asked his loyal companion while he walked over to the back door.

"Do you need to go outside?" Ryan asked as he opened the door. Buford just stared at him and barked again. "Really?" Ryan scoffed. "It's that bad?" Buford ran over to Ryan and nuzzled up against his leg. He waited for the command.

"OK, go get your leash," Ryan ordered. Buford darted over to his toy bin to fetch his leash. "We'll get a lap in before the pizza arrives," Ryan said happily. Buford and fresh air always cheered Ryan up. They headed to the north part of his property and around the southern trail.

Chapter 3

Ryan arrived in Sugar Grove just past noon about an hour earlier than he had intended. He didn't want to appear eager to be home, so he drove around the town and then instinctively to North Pole. Ryan drove onto the property and read the name of the street out loud to Buford incredulously, "Santa Claus Lane." He found out later they renamed the road to the factory, the Gift Store, and the Events Center right after Joe had died. The whole town had come out to the naming celebration. Joe was so beloved in the community. Naming the entrance road after Santa Claus fit the North Pole theme more than using Joe's name. It was appropriate, but it made Ryan sad – as if Grandpa were no longer a part of the legacy of the company though there was a heritage room in the Events Center that told Joe's life story. The main gate was open as always with no guard in sight. Crime was low in Sugar Grove, and

Grandpa Joe hadn't wanted the beautiful acreage to be wasted, so they built parks and athletic fields surrounding the factory. They even created a nature walk with several bridges over the creek that ran through the land. It was a scenic and peaceful environment. Families would come to have picnics. Sports leagues used the fields. Organizations in the community used the property and the Events Center for conferences and special parties. There always seemed to be somebody on campus, just as Grandpa Joe had wanted.

Ryan passed some hockey teams using the rinks and drove around to the back of the property where the nature trail started. He asked Buford if he wanted to go for a run. Buford leapt out of the car window before Ryan had even fully stopped the car. He had driven his red Corvette home, and Ryan double checked the paint by the passenger side window to make sure Buford hadn't scratched the body in his haste. He let Buford off the leash, though he carried it with him, and the two of them headed down the trail – a perfect way to spend 20 minutes before he headed over to his mother's. When he reached the last bridge, he stopped and looked over the incredible view of the factory and the surrounding area. He contemplated the past several years of his life and marveled again how his father and grandfather had dedicated their entire careers to this candy company and the village. It really was a gorgeous property. It was also a very profitable company that provided many altruistic benefits for the community. Why did he want nothing to do with it? At least he hadn't until recently.

Thirty minutes later Ryan pulled into the Miller estate. He had forgotten how pretty the entrance was during the daylight. He almost always arrived home at night and was gone by the next day. He hadn't seen this view in years. The driveway was lined with gorgeous, fully decorated pine trees donned with thousands of lights ready to be turned on at sundown. Next to each tree was a giant candy cane. Each one displayed a different printed message of Christmas cheer. It was a bit ridiculous to Ryan, but his mother and his sister were both infected with the family disease, Christmas Mania, so it was certainly no surprise to see the elaborate entrance decked out like an amusement park. There was also a fictional road sign along the driveway that said South Pole, a clever touch Ryan's father had added a year or so after the honor of Santa Claus Lane was given to the North Pole.

There was a large parking area in front of the barn where six vintage cars lined up as if they were waiting for a car rally. Buying sports cars was a hobby Ryan shared with his father. The barn doubled as an entertainment venue, and over the years they had allowed many people to get married on their property. They also had live music and dancing once a month. Jennifer managed that responsibility since she was home with her children. Near the home garage, Ryan recognized Jennifer's van and his mother's SUV. They were parked next to an old Honda Accord he recognized instantly as Heather's 2005 navy blue relic, which had to have over 300,000 miles on it by now. Ryan laughed out loud as he pulled up next to the Honda, and then butterflies soared in his stomach as he and Buford exited the car and headed toward the front door.

The Miller log cabin, made of beautiful pine, looked more like a resort than a house. It had three different levels, each accented with a sharp triangular point that jutted out between the majestic eastern white pines, several of which were well over 100 feet tall. Ryan's dad had designed and helped build the home right after Ryan was born. The house had been featured in magazines, used as a backdrop in advertisements, and occasionally tourists drove by to see it or take pictures. His parents never considered a no trespassing sign. They welcomed the visitors and often had conversations with them when they walked around the property. Ryan thought such folks were crazy and resented their intrusions when he lived there.

Before they made it to the stately porch, Ryan's niece and nephew flew out of the double doors and ran to see them. They greeted Buford first with big hugs, which Buford returned with a shower of licks and kisses. Ryan waited his turn for their hugs and understood their choice in first greeting. Buford, who acted as if the kids were the only friends he had ever known, was a better relative than he was. Ryan spoiled his niece and nephew with a gift every time he visited, so they looked at him with expectant eyes and eager nods. Ryan played it cool, milking the moment, until he knew it was driving them nearly crazy.

"Can you guys take Buford for a quick walk around the house?" Ryan asked coyly as they frowned in disappointment. They grabbed the leash Ryan offered them but looked at Ryan wistfully and didn't move a muscle.

"Well, before you take Buford for a walk," Ryan continued, as he took back the leash and popped the trunk on the Corvette, "there is something for each of you in the trunk."

When the kids heard the trunk pop, they left Ryan and sprinted to the car. As Ryan watched the children pull out their presents, Jennifer joined him on the sidewalk with a big homecoming hug for her big brother.

"Make sure your mother and dad are OK with those," Ryan shouted over his shoulder, while both kids held up a Nintendo Switch and screamed for joy.

"You make Christmas time very difficult for Gabe and me, Ryan," Jennifer said laughing, though there was a sad truth in her sentiment.

"I know," Ryan said, "but I'm a lousy uncle, so at least I can buy them some cool things once in a while."

Jennifer did not disagree or counter his statement. Ryan *was* a lousy uncle. He barely knew her children's names, and he rarely showed interest in any of their hobbies or passions. He hadn't been to any of Tucker's baseball games or hockey tournaments. Tucker was obsessed with baseball, and like his Uncle Ryan, was a pretty good player. He was playing up at the U10 level even though he had just turned nine. He was also a good hockey player, his team often playing in tournaments on North Pole's rinks. Gabby loved dance, ice skating, and horses, but Ryan had never seen her ride or perform in any show though he was always invited. It wasn't that Ryan didn't want to come, but his Saturdays included office work, so he could never make it home in time on a weeknight to attend anything. Jennifer often reminded him that he was the CEO and could make the rules for his company and certainly, at the very least, decide how he spent his own time. She also knew that Ryan was just like her father and actually enjoyed his long hours and the tough work. Both men also took care of their employees and made sure the key employees had the time off they needed, even if it came at their own expense. It's why the separation between Jim and Ryan made Jennifer and Becky so mad and sad. The two men were so much alike!

When the kids came back around the barn, they all went inside together. Ryan gave a handshake to Gabe and a long hug to his mother. She was the only one who received Ryan's true affection; she was the only person he really trusted. Becky was also a fantastic cook and enjoyed making his favorite dishes. Ryan took his bags to his room and tried to look for Heather without being obvious. He didn't see her anywhere but figured she had to be somewhere on site if her car was in the driveway. He splashed some water on his face and made sure his hair looked decent before heading back downstairs. He also grabbed a bag out of his backpack and hoped he wouldn't be overstepping his bounds with a gift he had for Henry.

The dining room table was set like a Christmas post card, like a scene out of a Hallmark movie, with the centerpiece a gingerbread replica of the original North Pole factory. There were an assortment of North Pole's famous Christmas candies at every setting and a large candy cane on each plate. Every year North Pole created a new flavor of candy cane for the Christmas season, almost always their number-one seller of the year. This year's flavor was caramel hot chocolate. Jennifer snatched up Tucker's and Gabby's before they were unwrapped and sampled. Ryan stuck his candy cane in the inside lining of his sports coat. He hoped he'd remember to take it out later and give it to Buford, who had an enormous sweet tooth. Ryan stopped eating candy after Joe died, though his own sweet tooth in his youth was legendary. It was his private defiance to the ill-fated passing of his hero.

There were enough spaces at dinner for more than the family, so Ryan assumed Heather was joining them.

"Who else is joining us for lunch, Mom?" Ryan asked as cool and calmly as he could.

"The prettiest woman not named Jennifer in Sugar Grove," Becky, beaming, confidently bragged.

Ryan turned away to avoid a smile with his mother, but Jennifer caught it and enjoyed teasing her perfectionistic, protective, and private older brother.

"Heather is coming in a little while with Henry. Her car broke down and she is borrowing one of mom's until she can get Old Faithful running again or finally decides to buy a new one." Old Faithful was the name Jennifer had given Heather's car back in college, and it had certainly lived up to its name. During one argument with Ryan, Heather had compared Old Faithful to Ryan in a detailed rant full of characteristics, abilities, and loyalty. Old Faithful won the competition rather easily. It still stung Ryan a bit, though he appreciated the dramatic and passionate argument from Heather and couldn't stop a wry grin when Jennifer used the moniker.

"I bet you are super excited to see her again, aren't you, brother?" Jennifer pestered. "She is as beautiful and fun as ever, but she is still too good for you." The last line came out a little mean-spirited, but Jennifer was also being honest.

"She can't wait to see you," Becky shouted from the island, saving Ryan from more teasing. "She said it's been about five years since you guys have seen each other or talked," Becky continued. "I think that's crazy."

"She was married, Mom," Ryan retorted, annoyed. "Most husbands prefer that their wives not hold regular conversations with other men, especially ex-boyfriends."

Jennifer sided with Ryan this time. "He has a point, Mom, especially since Ryan was way more than just an ex-boyfriend."

"But she's been divorced for over a year now, Ryan," Becky said sadly. "Why in the world would you not check in on her, see how she was doing? It's been a tough year."

Ryan started to offer a pathetic excuse when Heather and Henry walked through the front hallway and into the kitchen. The whole room turned in rapt attention to watch the first eye contact between the two people the whole town thought should have married. Heather had heard the last part of Becky's challenge and was embarrassed and turning red as she greeted her.

"I'm pretending I didn't hear any of that last conversation," Heather said to everybody as she entered the great room.

Ryan instinctively backed his seat from the table and stood up to greet her, but Heather ignored him and went right to Becky without glancing his way. She had brought some fruit and veggies for the lunch and, though she hated to admit it, she was way more nervous to see Ryan than she had originally anticipated. Becky could tell she was nervous and immediately asked her about work to diffuse the tension. Henry ran over to see Gabby. He was just a year younger than his friend, and the two played well together. Ryan had never seen Henry in person, so he stared awkwardly and tried not to think about the fact that he could have a son or children that same age. He also kept an eye on Heather and was easily, once again, captivated by her looks, spirit, and energy. The fact that she was single and in his presence began to dawn on him, and his hands started to perspire.

After a few minutes of socially polite small talk, Ryan engaged in conversation with Henry. "Henry, if it's alright with your mother, I have something for you," Ryan said a little too boldly. The table paused to watch Heather and listen to what she would say.

Ryan continued, "Every time I visit Tucker and Gabby, I bring them a fun gift. I thought I might get to see you this week, so I bought something for you also." As he finished his explanation, he glanced over at Heather, who was neither smiling nor amused. And the truth was, he didn't pick out the gifts and never did. His assistant, Tammy, did all his shopping for him. He had never disclosed this to his family, but he was pretty sure they knew.

"Well, I guess that will be fine, Ryan," Heather said without gratitude or thanksgiving. "Henry, Honey, Ryan is Gabby's uncle, and it's OK to receive a present from him." She directed Henry from the island 10 feet away, so her volume and tone were sharp.

"OK, Mom," Henry said and timidly took the bag from Ryan.

Henry pulled out his Nintendo Switch and celebrated the unexpected gift. "Wow. So cool. Thanks a ton," he exclaimed.

Ryan smiled with relief.

"Mom, look at what I got!" Henry said to Heather.

"Wow, that's really cool, Henry. What do you tell Gabby's uncle?"

"Thank you, sir," Henry said with pure joy in his eyes as he looked lovingly at Ryan.

"You are quite welcome, Henry," Ryan replied. "I used to know your mother a long time ago" – he paused and should have quit talking, but he didn't – "but we had some tough times and couldn't work through some tough decisions, so we haven't seen each other in a while."

It was way more information than was needed, and the whole table stared at Ryan in confusion and disbelief. Jennifer was flabbergasted but remembered

Ryan had really never been around children. She prayed Heather would think of that fact also.

"Like my dad?" Henry, his huge brown eyes wide open, asked Ryan.

Ryan had no idea how to reply and glanced helplessly at Jennifer, who kept quiet, and then looked over his shoulder to Becky or Heather for help. A few seconds that felt like eternity passed.

"No, Honey," Heather explained, rescuing Ryan. "Uncle Ryan and I were not married, and we did not get divorced. We were really good friends for many years, but then he moved to the Twin Cities."

"OK," Henry, satisfied with his mother's explanation, said. "Can I play with the Nintendo now?"

"No, not till after lunch. You may play with it whenever Gabby is allowed to play with hers." From her comments, Ryan surmised Heather was a pretty authoritative mother.

"OK, Mom. Thanks again, sir," the adorable little boy said to Ryan.

Ryan was glad Heather had bailed him out of the inappropriate self-disclosure, but he knew she was mad and would have a hard time not reprimanding him at some point. He hoped it was after lunch. No such luck.

"Ryan," Heather said sharply as she approached the table and leaned over near Ryan's ear and away from everyone's direction. "May I speak with you outside for a minute before we eat?" Ryan knew this was not really a request and quietly pushed himself away from the table.

"Sure," Ryan stammered and excused himself, and the former couple, seven years removed, tensely walked down the hallway and out the front door for privacy while Jennifer, Gabe, and Becky all looked at each other anxiously.

Chapter 3

"That didn't take long," Jennifer said with obvious disappointment.

"I think it is good," Becky countered. "Heather can teach Ryan some basic fundamentals of parenting." She used general communication, the three children at the table having stopped talking to watch the fascinating adult interactions.

Chapter 4

Heather started in on Ryan before they had even made it off the porch.

"Ryan, I don't know where to begin." Heather paced back and forth blocking the stairway, which Ryan wanted to descend to avoid this uncomfortable scenario. "And how can you make me so mad, so quickly?" Heather asked rhetorically. Ryan wisely didn't answer. "You always could," Heather acknowledged to both of them, taking a few deep breaths.

Ryan still did not speak and simply waited for her to continue. Heather was an external processor and usually talked through her feelings, but Ryan was such an internal processor she knew she needed to give a direct message. If she simply gave a passionate rant, he could miss the point.

Stopping her pacing and turning to face Ryan, Heather moved closer to avoid yelling and making a scene and stepped close to his body. They were nearly face to face. There were tears in her eyes and her emotional response caught Ryan off guard. He wanted to back away but knew he couldn't.

"Ryan, you can't march in here after five years of ignoring me and Henry and bring him an expensive gift. I appreciate your generosity, though I doubt you did the actual shopping, but Henry doesn't even know who you are. You weren't present. . . ." Heather continued, nearly rehashing several past wounds, but stopped herself. "You haven't been a part of our lives." Ryan knew she wasn't finished yet and again kept silent, still maintaining eye contact. Heather continued, with conviction, "And even more importantly, please don't have adult conversations with a five-year-old about anything, let alone our past relationship. Henry's having a really difficult time missing his father and you just added to his heartache."

Chapter 4

When they were dating, Ryan and Heather were terrible at managing conflict. Their different personalities and temperaments were a strength during everyday conversations, but when disagreement entered the picture, it drove a wedge between them, their issues never resolved, and their fights often went on for hours or days. This time, however, especially since it involved Heather's child, Ryan didn't defend, debate, or deflect. He actually took a step closer toward Heather. He could smell her perfume and feel her breath.

"I am truly sorry, Heather," Ryan said gently, gazing right into her moistened green eyes. "I have no idea how to talk to children and I'm . . . a little overwhelmed with all of this," he disclosed, waving his arms over his head.

Though not a grand level of self-disclosure, this was an enormous vulnerability for a man who normally revealed nothing. This genuine expression spoke to the lasting intimacy of their relationship, even if it had lain dormant for seven years. Both of them felt the connection instantly and had an awkward moment of tenderness. Ryan found himself wanting to kiss her or hug her. He didn't dare act on it, but he wondered if his thoughts were apparent in his eyes.

Heather finally stepped back a bit, wiped her tears, and said with a little surprise in her voice, "Thank you, Ryan. Please communicate with me about anything you want to say or do with Henry in the future. And we are just as overwhelmed with this as you are. Your father was a second dad to me, and, really, was Henry's primary father figure the last two years. This is a huge loss for all of us."

Now it was Ryan's turn for tears to formulate, though he didn't let them fall. It was, however, the first emotional response that had surfaced regarding the passing of his father, and his bottom lip suddenly began to quiver. Heather, moved by Ryan's vulnerability, and in true nature to her relational style, moved forward and wrapped Ryan in her arms. "I'm so sorry your dad passed," she said warmly. Ryan didn't respond verbally but sunk into her care. He didn't let go of Heather right away, and she reciprocated the intensity of the affection. *Maybe there were two women who really cared about me*, Ryan thought to himself.

"Thanks," he finally offered as he tenderly released her, their hands touching for a moment. "Sorry, that was a long hug, but I really needed that." They stared at each other with surprising intimacy and both blushed.

"That's OK," Heather offered with a smile. "I think I needed it also." Their eyes remained glued on each other. "We should probably get inside for lunch," she finally opined, interrupting the gaze by looking toward the door. "Jennifer is probably on her way to the porch."

They both headed back into the house where Jennifer was indeed walking down the hallway toward their location. "Everything alright with you two?" she asked with a relieved tone, seeing no continued animosity in their body language.

"Just cleared up a few boundaries," Heather stated emphatically, and both she and Ryan smiled widely at Jennifer as they walked by. Jennifer gave Heather an inquisitive look. The best friends would have to wait a while before full the former would hear the latter's confession.

The rest of the meal was uneventful other than how delicious it was and the fact that Ryan completely enjoyed himself. He tried not to look at Heather much, but their eyes caught multiple times, and he had a tough time looking away. He abided by the boundary Heather initiated with Henry, though he found himself in tune to all three children and gave a listening ear to responses Gabby and Tucker gave to Becky's questions about their latest endeavors. It became a challenge, however, to maintain that boundary when Henry captivated the table with a simple statement he made to Ryan.

"Uncle Ryan," Henry blurted out trying to get Ryan's attention.

Ryan looked at Heather first. He wondered what level of affirmation was needed for a simple conversation. Heather nodded in approval before Ryan acknowledged the inquiry from the youngster.

"Yes, Henry?" Ryan answered.

"You look a lot like Grandpa Jim. Did you know him? He was really nice."

The innocence of the statements froze the whole room. It also made Ryan extremely uncomfortable, and he shifted in his chair to maintain composure and summon the strength to answer simply and without tears. His mother and sister, with no move to bail him out, waited for him to answer.

'Yes, Henry. Jim was my dad," Ryan finally offered, doing a good job to keep the response simple, and everyone smiled in relief.

"Wow," Henry said with a big smile. "Same with me then," though no one understood exactly what he meant.

Ryan looked at Heather to see if he could or should ask what that meant. Heather gave Ryan a tilted head nonverbal cue along with her hand flashed forward, palm down, signifying to everyone she would finish the conversation.

"Same as what, Honey? How are you and Ryan the same?" Heather asked her only son.

"Uncle Ryan and I don't have our dads anymore," Henry said concisely and then smiled. He was thrilled with himself for the conditional association his sharp little mind had figured out. It was quite impressive.

Chapter 4

The family was amazed at Henry's perceptivity, and no one said a word, though Becky and Jennifer had tears rolling down their cheeks. Ryan looked down, fearing a second emotional response in less than an hour, unable to look at Heather for reinforcement or permission to speak.

Heather put closure on the powerful moment. "You are right, Honey. You and Ryan do have a lot in common." Then she looked at Becky who intervened appropriately.

"Besides the candy on the table, North Pole just produced their newest Christmas ice cream flavor, Mistletoe Mint. Who wants to try a scoop?" Everyone responded affirmatively.

****

After the table was cleared Ryan went out in the backyard with Buford to let him run around and to get a little time by himself. He had thoroughly enjoyed the meal with his family, but it was a lot of interpersonal interaction for him, and he was pretty tired. He still was blown away at Henry's statement and his understanding of loss. Ryan played fetch with Buford for 10 minutes and then went to sit by the fire pit, where he started an impressive fire. He pulled his cell phone out and started to look at his email and then stopped. He turned to Buford to consider the plight of his mental state.

"Buford, why do I want to check my email on a Sunday afternoon?" Buford gave Ryan the eye contact he needed to continue. "What is my problem, boy? Why can't I just relax? Unwind and unplug?" Buford now left his warm spot in the sun and nestled up close to his master. "You understand me, don't you, boy?" Buford put his head on Ryan's lap and enjoyed the consistent stroke from his nose to behind his ears. "Compulsive Email Observer," Ryan said to Buford while laughing at himself. After a few minutes contemplating his life and his future, someone came from behind and stroked his hair.

Chapter 4

"What are you thinking about, Ryan?" He knew before the question only his mother would rub his head – and he would only allow his mother to show that kind of public affection.

"Wondering what I am doing, Mom," Ryan said, more honestly than he intended. "I have everything I need, everything I want, and, honestly, everything I ever dreamed of having. . . . " But he didn't finish the obvious movement toward a lack of happiness or joy. Becky let the silence say what they both knew. Having been married to Ryan's father for over 50 years, she had known how to let her stubborn husband reach his own conclusions, and the same was true for her proud son. They were both wonderful leaders that were unafraid to take on massive responsibility and risks – and to use their name to better their communities – but they were also fiercely independent and sensitive men, who did not easily show emotion or vulnerability, weakness or dependence.

How she wished the two men would have reconciled. She stayed quiet, letting Ryan think, and took the seat next to him.

After another few minutes of silence, Jennifer and Heather came out to join the two of them, and they all enjoyed the fire and the beautiful nature around them. Gabe had taken the three kids down to the lake to look for winter toads that could survive the cold water and the nearly iced-over lake. Eventually, Jennifer punctured the serenity with a general question for either her mother or Heather.

"Who is going to run the North Pole contests this week?" Heather looked at Becky, who kept quiet, so she knew she could explain the new process in leadership.

"All of the executive officers are running different events," Heather shared. "We will each lead one of the five events, and Becky will help close out the final celebration."

Chapter 4

Ryan didn't know if he was more surprised by Heather's *We* or his mother's agreement to be a part of the grand finale: the Christmas Cookie Challenge. Jennifer beat him to the next question. "Which event will you run, Heather?"

"I plan to run the ice skating contest on Wednesday night," Heather said.

"You don't even like ice skating," Jennifer protested.

"As the rookie on the executive team, I didn't get a choice," Heather responded. "And I don't hate skating; there are just some tough memories around the ice." Besides the breakup with Ryan on the skating contest night, her parents' car accident was ice-related. They hit black ice, skidding off the road and into a tree, and were killed instantly.

"VP of Human Resources." Ryan broke the sad silence and said it more to himself than to Heather.

"That's right," Becky said, "and she has done an excellent job." And with that affirmation, she rose to her feet, patted Ryan's knee, and gave him a wink before she continued. "I'm going in to rest for a while. It sure is good to have my children, all of my children," she said while looking at Heather, "home with me during this Christmas season."

"OK, Mom," Jennifer responded. "Heather and I are heading into town to buy some presents. Gabe and Ryan can watch the kids." She said this with a big grin and looked at Ryan for his reaction.

Ryan looked at Heather who was looking at him. "I'd be glad to," Ryan said sheepishly, "if Heather is OK with it."

"That would be great, Ryan," she replied. "Thank you. I really need some time alone to finish shopping. Henry is used to being with Gabe and Tucker. He won't give you any trouble."

Chapter 4

"OK," Ryan said. "He doesn't seem like the kind of kid to give anybody any trouble. Should I go down to the lake and find them?"

"No," Jennifer answered. "Gabe let me know they are on their way back. The kids want to drink some hot chocolate and watch a movie in the basement." There was a large theatre-styled room in the basement.

"Alright, sounds good," Ryan said. "You ladies have a good time. I'll head in with you and get the hot chocolate started. Could they have some popcorn also?"

"That would be great," Jennifer said, a bit surprised.

"Popcorn is Henry's favorite treat," Heather affirmed.

"Like mother, like son," Ryan noted, smiling at Heather. He was proud of himself for being free in conversation and for remembering Heather' favorite snack food. The three of them climbed up the deck stairs and through the sliding door into the kitchen, where Becky had laid out the hot chocolate choices before retiring to her room.

****

While Jennifer and Heather walked to the car, Jennifer stated the obvious. "There is still some chemistry between you two, isn't there?"

"Who? Ryan and me?" Heather asked unconvincingly.

"Yes, of course," Jennifer implored, "and you know it." Heather conveniently reached for her seat belt, which allowed her to avoid Jennifer's stare. Jennifer continued as both girls giggled. "My brother is different around you. He would never have agreed to watch the kids with Gabe if you and Henry weren't around. I think you need to spend a bunch of time with us this week."

"Maybe we will," Heather said shyly, "for you, your mom and the kids, of course," and both ladies laughed at this inauthentic declaration.

Chapter 5

Ryan had three hot chocolates full of North Pole marshmallows waiting for the kids when they returned. They were cold and wet, but they had caught several toads – and even named them Ryan, Heather, and Jennifer – before Gabe made Tucker release them back into their natural habitat.

"What movie are we going to watch?" Ryan asked as they munched on the popcorn and drank their hot chocolates.

"Are you watching with us?" Tucker asked Ryan with surprised anticipation.

"Are you guys good with that?" Ryan asked.

Gabe choked a bit on his hot chocolate in shock but passed it off as going down his windpipe. Ryan hadn't watched TV with the kids since they were babies. He always disappeared to work on his computer during quiet times and around family celebrations.

"Yeah," all three kids shouted in unconditional affirmation.

Ryan hated to admit it, but three children who wanted him to watch an animated movie with them made him very happy.

"I get to sit on Uncle Ryan's lap," Henry claimed. Ryan looked at Gabe to register the appropriateness of this request. Gabe intervened as Gabby gave a strong visceral response of emphatic growling to indicate her territorial rights to her aloof uncle, who was apparently now available for snuggles.

"Henry, you will get lap time with Uncle Ryan, but we will allow Gabby the first half hour," Gabe instructed. "Does that sound fine?"

"Awesome," Henry said, and the three kids raced down the stairs to claim their favorite spots on the giant, sectional couch. It didn't matter where you sat. The view was not obstructed or altered because the screen was 10 feet by 10 feet and there weren't any poor angles or sightlines.

Ryan started to clean up the messy table, and Gabe couldn't help but comment on the apparent changes in the man he used to know as his brother-in-law.

"Thanks, Ryan, for spending some time with the kids. They will talk about this all day. All week, in fact. They really do think you're cool, you know." Ryan remained quiet and kept cleaning. Gabe continued, "They just want to love you and know you." Gabe let his voice trail off, assuming he had probably shared a bit too deeply for Ryan, but instead of getting angry or walking away – two normal responses Ryan had to family accountability or disclosure in the past – Ryan looked at Gabe and apologized.

"Gabe, you are right, and I am sorry. I have not been a good uncle to your children or a good brother-in-law to you, and that is going to change. It might take me a while, but I am committed to becoming more involved in their lives if you and Jennifer give me another chance. And I'm not talking about just buying them things, either." Ryan stopped himself, but he realized he could have kept talking. He smiled to no one in particular and then finished putting the dishes in the sink. "Let's go watch the movie. The kids are waiting for us."

Gabe said he would be right down but first needed to go to the restroom. He didn't. He lied. He had to run to the backroom and FaceTime Jennifer. "I don't know what has gotten into your brother," he exclaimed before even saying hello. "Ryan just talked about getting involved in our lives, in the kids' lives, and becoming a better uncle. And he meant it. I could see it. It wasn't just talk. Something is happening to him." Gabe stopped and was thrilled at how happy his news was making his wife, apparent from the joy all over her face.

Chapter 5

"I'll tell you what is happening," Jennifer cooed, turning her phone so that Heather's face was in the screen. "Heather is happening," she squealed.

"What?" Heather proclaimed coyly. "I have nothing to do with this," she said innocently but while smiling from ear to ear.

"Well, whatever it is," Gabe said happily, "it's about time – and all three kids are eating it up. They just had a debate about who could sit on Ryan's lap for the movie."

Now it was Jennifer's turn for unbelief. "What? That is great. Did you let Gabby go first?" Jennifer asked hopefully with a semi-stern look.

"Sure did, Honey, and if I wouldn't have, the future North Pole executive would have fought for it," Gabe replied, laughing. "She actually growled about her rights to her uncle!"

"She gets that side of her personality from your family," Jennifer said sarcastically.

"Heather, is it OK if Henry takes a turn on Ryan's lap?" Gabe asked loudly enough for Heather to hear amidst the Christmas carols blasting through the speakers in the mall.

"Does he want to?" Heather asked curiously.

"He was the one who brought the whole subject up in the first place," Gabe, astounded, affirmed. "My kids wouldn't have asked Ryan because it hasn't happened before."

"Wow," Heather said with a dramatic pause. "Sure. I guess that is fine with me. He must feel connected to Ryan through Jim. Usually, he is not that warm and open to men."

"Maybe he is reading the heart of his mother," Jennifer said with sincerity, and both ladies were silent for a second. "Gabe?" Jennifer finally asked.

"Yes, Honey?" Gabe responded.

"I think you need to get downstairs and join the movie," Jennifer said playfully.

Chapter 5

"Oh, that's right. Sorry. I forgot!" Gabe ended the call without saying goodbye and ran down the stairway to join the others.

When Gabe walked around the corner of the basement, he was amazed at the scene. Gabby was proudly on Ryan's lap in her favorite blanket, holding Ryan's arm firmly, which she had draped around herself. Henry was nestled into Ryan's other side and using Ryan's ribs as his pillow. He had Ryan's other arm around his body and down to his legs and was playing with Ryan's fingers while he watched. They were literally "tucked in" with Uncle Ryan. Even Tucker was closer to Ryan than Gabe had ever seen him. Gabe gave Ryan a raised eyebrow's glance, and Ryan shrugged his shoulders with an innocent smile in response. Gabe took the other section of the couch, and Buford jumped up next to him for company. Buford, not pleased to share his master with the children, jealously gave his affection to Gabe for the remainder of the movie.

That evening, Becky prepared another wonderful meal after which they agreed to drive through Sugar Grove and see the Christmas lights. Sugar Grove was a destination sight for Christmas lights every year, so it was an annual tradition for the four surrounding counties. The children rode in Gabe and Jennifer's minivan, and Heather and Becky rode with Ryan in one of Jim's, and now Becky's, extra cars since Ryan's Corvette was only a two-seater. They rode through the town and enjoyed the sights with Becky narrating commentary of all the local news and gossip for Ryan and Heather. Normally this kind of small town talk annoyed Ryan, who found it trivial and unnecessary. Today, however, he felt rested and attentive and even asked some follow-up questions and points of clarification, finding himself slightly interested in the news. He couldn't believe how many people from his youth still lived in the community. For the first time in a decade, he felt some nostalgia and some hometown pride as the village was decked head to toe in Christmas glory. It really was bright and merry. *Maybe this is what community is supposed to feel like*, Ryan reflected.

When they reached the end of town and turned around in the high school parking lot, Becky received a call from the other van. Grandma's presence was requested by Gabby, and she was not taking no for an answer. Grandma gladly obliged and jumped out of the front seat of the car before Heather or Ryan could object. She opened the back door, telling Heather to get in the front seat, and whisked away to the waiting grandkids. Heather closed the back door, glanced at the front of her alma mater briefly, took a deep breath, and slid into the front seat under the watchful eye of the entire minivan. She shut the door softly and buckled up before she dared to look at Ryan. This felt like one of their first dates all over again. Ryan's heartbeat raced and he wanted to reach for her hand and tell her how much he missed her, but he was too nervous to say anything other than "Ready?"

"Absolutely," Heather replied.

Ryan gently turned the car in the right direction and toward the main road again and the van followed in line. "Are you warm enough?" he asked her.

"Yep, doing fine," Heather answered way too quickly. Both professional communicators were struggling to find any organic conversation, so they drove in awkward silence for several minutes.

Ryan started to panic that he was blowing a major chance to reconnect with his first and only love when Heather broke the ice and opened the floor for them both. "It sure is good to see you again."

"I was just going to tell you that," Ryan affirmed, returning the compliment affectionately, and the two friends talked politely about life and career during the 15-minute ride home, which ended way too soon. As they pulled in the driveway Ryan, emboldened by the atmosphere and environment, became more assertive with Heather. He parked the car and shifted quickly in his seat so he could face Heather.

"Heather, before you get out of the car, could I ask you something?" Ryan said very officially.

"Sure," Heather replied a bit nervously. Her voice almost cracked with a combination of anxiousness and surprise.

Ryan then paused for a few seconds to gather himself and to strengthen the nerve he needed to proceed while the van pulled in next to them. "Would it be alright if I see you and Henry again this week sometime? Or do you have commitments all week due to the North Pole contests? I understand if you're too busy. Or, if you don't think we should. Or if you just don't want to." The polished CEO was communicating like a schoolboy asking his crush to the prom.

Ryan turned away sheepishly, embarrassed by his rambling request. Heather couldn't keep herself from laughing and felt bad that she obviously bruised Ryan's ego temporarily. It all was worth it when Heather gained her composure and spoke.

"I'd like that," she said with a big smile. "Actually, I think we'd like that," pointing past Ryan and toward Henry, who was out of the van and heading over to Ryan's side of the car.

"Great," Ryan said. "Fantastic." He smiled broadly. "What can we do tomorrow night?" Before Heather could answer, Henry knocked on the window. When Ryan rolled it down, Henry took care of the question for both of them.

"Mom, Mom!" Henry exclaimed.

"Yes, dear?" Heather replied.

"Can Ryan come with us tomorrow night to the snowman contest?" Henry begged.

Chapter 5

"Of course, he can, son," Heather responded and looked at Ryan for confirmation.

"I would love to, Henry," Ryan said happily, "but I need to warn you that I won that competition with my dad a couple of times when I was your age, so we have to build to win." Becky and Jennifer had joined the group, and both ladies smiled when they heard the phrase Jim often used with Ryan now being used by Ryan with Henry.

"Awesome!" Henry proclaimed. "Mom, can Ryan come over to our house tomorrow afternoon to practice before the contest? Please? Please?" he implored.

"It's OK with me if it's good with him," Heather affirmed.

"It's a date then," Ryan said, and the rest of the family took advantage of Ryan's word choice to immediately razz the vulnerable executive. Gabby, ever precocious and romantically inclined, teased her uncle.

"Uncle Ryan has a date with Heather and Ryan!" She repeated the sing-song pronouncement several times.

Gabe intervened for his brother-in-law by shifting from love to competition. "We'll see you guys at the contest," pointing at the car where Ryan, Heather, and Henry were. "We have been practicing for this event for months." Gabby growled again, this time in mock family pride.

"Ryan," Heather then said stoically, "you need to get out of the car now. This is the car your mother is letting us borrow and we need to get home." Everyone had another good laugh at Ryan's expense.

"Of course. Of course." Ryan quickly jumped out of the car and then raced around the back to finish opening Heather's partially opened door.

"Wow. What a gentleman." Heather blushed and immediately felt the eyes of the rest of the family on them both. Ryan walked her arm and arm to the driver's side door and ushered her into the driver's seat.

"If we have a date tomorrow," Ryan put forth, playfully continuing the mood, "we have to start the gentlemanly behavior tonight."

The family clapped in approval, and for a moment Heather and Ryan froze in arm-holding tandem as Henry let himself into the back of the car and shut the door for himself.

"See you tomorrow," Ryan finally said, reluctantly releasing Heather's arm. He could have easily walked her home and encouraged Henry to drive himself back if it had meant more time with his forever love – and if the police wouldn't have arrested him for endangering a child.

Ryan watched the car drive away before he turned around to face the peanut gallery.

"What a gentleman," Jennifer teased, imitating Heather's tone and hair flip. Gabe added, "Seems like you really do have a date tomorrow night, Ryan."

Ryan didn't deny it and instead continued the competitive spirit Gabe had introduced earlier. "A date to take the snowman championship!" Ryan yelled as he slapped Gabe on the shoulder and made his way up the sidewalk. "Let's go have some more hot chocolate and popcorn," he bellowed, bounding up the steps and into the house.

"Yeah!" the kids echoed as they jogged to catch up with their now playful uncle and the always playful Buford, who had run out of the house when Ryan entered and now followed the kids back inside.

Becky leaned over to Jennifer and whispered, "Isn't this wonderful? Ryan and Heather together again." They both nodded and smiled and joined the men and the kids in the house.

Chapter 6

Ryan and Heather agreed to meet around 2:00. That would give them an hour to practice their snowman techniques before eating dinner and heading to the North Pole. Ryan worked all morning and only surfaced in the great room around lunch. Gabe was at work. He was a fifth grade schoolteacher at Country Knoll Elementary School. He had taught there for ten years, and the students loved him. He had his master's degree and the school wanted him to move into administration, but he wasn't quite ready to leave the classroom yet. The last day of school was Wednesday the 22nd and, with missing Tuesday for the funeral, Gabe didn't want to miss that Monday morning, as well. Jennifer and the kids were at home, so it was just lunch with Ryan and his mother. The house was really quiet.

Becky was a little reserved as she brought Ryan his chili and crackers. She wasn't down, just contemplative, and Ryan didn't pry right away, so they ate their chili together silently. They enjoyed their mutual-introvert company together, but after a few minutes, Ryan, clearing the table for her, finally inquired as to the source of her contemplation.

"You doing OK, Mom? You're a little extra quiet," Ryan initiated.

"The start of Christmas competition week brought up a lot of memories for me, Ryan. Your father really loved this week. He looked forward to it all year long. The last few years he even let his beard grow and wore the Santa suit just as Grandpa did," Becky shared. "Did you know that, Honey?"

"I remember the picture you sent me a couple of years ago, but I didn't know he was wearing it all the time. Did he even wear it to work as Grandpa did?" Ryan wondered.

"He sure did, Sweetie. And the kids in the village responded to him just like they did Grandpa Joe.

It's the spirit in the heart that reflects Santa, not the body in the suit." Becky gave this explanation because unlike Joe, who was built pretty similar to the prototypical Santa Claus, Jim was tall and thin, as was Ryan.

Ryan switched gears since he had his mother to himself for a moment. He surprised her with his vulnerable question. "Why wasn't Dad proud of me, Mom? Why couldn't he accept that I wanted to be a CEO of my own company, not the North Pole?" Ryan's voice was soft and reflective and absent of accusation; he really wanted to know.

"Honey," Becky said with a mother's empathy, "your father was very proud of you. He bragged about your business and accomplishments to everyone. He would follow your deals and activities through the *Minnesota Daily* online. He was hurt because he thought you believed the North Pole wasn't good enough for you and that what he and grandpa had dedicated their lives to was not worthy of your passions and talent. That really ate at him. No matter how many times I explained to him you needed to prove yourself somewhere else first, he took it personally that you wouldn't come back home and join him, learn from him."

Ryan was sad, but the truth from his mother – without the presence of his father –allowed him to receive what many times prior he had been unable to accept. This wasn't the first time his mother had explained to him the issue from his father's perspective, but this time it penetrated his heart differently. "I knew he respected me, Mom. I just needed to hear that he was proud of me – that he was impressed with what I was able to do on my own, without having the family business handed to me," Ryan explained, articulating his side of the issue. "But lately, Mom, all my success doesn't mean much to me. It's starting to feel a little empty, a little alone."

Chapter 6

"I understand, Honey," Becky said, giving him a pat on the hand, "but part of the problem is that you have never really shared it with us." She continued, going right to the heart of the matter and of the moment, "I think it's also about time for you to find a wife and settle down. I want some more grandkids before I get too old."

Every previous time his mother had hinted at marriage or kids, Ryan would rebuke her and move on to another topic quickly. This time he did not. "I think you are right, Mom, and I know you always believed Heather and I should be together. After being with her just a few times the last few days, I think I might agree."

"Speaking of Heather," his mother replied, suddenly becoming noticeably excited and happy, "what time are you supposed to go to Heather's?"

"2:00," Ryan answered, and then his phone ringer went off. Fittingly, the ringtone was "Under Pressure," the song from the band Queen. It was

Tammy. Ryan groaned and apologized to his mom. "Sorry, Mom. Thanks for lunch and talking with me, but I need to take this. It's my office manager."

"I understand, Honey," Becky said with a smile. "I was married to a CEO, you know."

"Thanks," Ryan told her as he said hello to Tammy and walked into the great room.

The phone call from Tammy was not good news. No, it was actually great news, but it was terrible news at this exact moment, especially in regard to his date with Heather and Henry. Mark Davidson, the CEO from Minnesota Industrial Incorporated (MII), the Fortune 500 company Emerging Enterprises had just merged with, had been frantically attempting to reach Ryan the past 24 hours and finally caught Tammy thirty minutes prior, when she showed up at Emerging's offices. Ryan hadn't received a voice mail, email, or text since the fire pit, and now he recognized why. Sometimes Ryan's cell reception in Sugar Grove was pretty weak, another issue that usually irritated him about his hometown, though this time it had given him a much needed day to unplug. MII wanted to add a few additional initiatives with Emerging based on a very favorable response from the announcement in the *New York Times* and the stock response that followed. They wanted Ryan to read a 30-page proposal they had put together over the weekend and to give them a counterproposal with agreement conditions by the end of the week – by Christmas Eve.

Normally, this kind of news from Tammy would have provided a surge of exhilaration and energy for Ryan and help solidify his "Bah! Humbug!" spirit during the Christmas season. These additional initiatives would potentially be worth tens of millions for Emerging and likely another million for Ryan himself. But not now – not this week, when he was on vacation and when he had to bury his father. And more specifically, not when he was focused on rekindling a romance with the only woman he had ever loved. The timing couldn't have been worse. Ryan told Tammy to ask for an extra week and paced around the room thinking through his options. He needed the week after Christmas to make this happen. It would be beneficial to be back in his office, alone, where he always worked best after hours or on the weekend. But for once, he didn't want to do that. Tammy called back 15 minutes later and shared that Mark had agreed to the extra seven days for the full counterproposal and agreement conditions, but they needed the initial proposal read and confirmed as a viable business plan tonight. Ryan had no choice. He accepted the timeframe and began reading the downloaded proposal Tammy had sent through his email, which had finally connected to the South Pole Wi-Fi.

At 1:40 p.m., Becky came into the room to check on him. "Honey, it's twenty till two. You have to leave in five minutes to be on time for Heather's."

Chapter 6

"Oh, no!" Ryan had buried himself in work mode and completely forgotten about the snowman practice let alone the snowman competition later that night. "Mom, would you call Heather and tell her I'm sorry, but I can't make it." Ryan simply glanced at his mom as he did when directing Tammy without giving her the benefit of context.

"Absolutely not, Ryan. This is your commitment issue to work through. This news will not go over well," Becky said sharply and with some disappointment.

"Mom!" Ryan pleaded like a teenager.

"No chance," Becky said. "Good luck with the call. You realize that Heather took time off from North Pole to give Henry this opportunity with you?"

Ryan finally looked up from his computer as the weight of his decision registered. "She did?" Ryan asked, hoping it wasn't true.

"She sure did, Honey. And remember she is a VP now. She assuredly rearranged many duties and responsibilities," Becky countered, with a touch of feminine pride in Heather's role and some frustration that Ryan had assumed Heather was free and available.

Ryan, silent and dejected, offered a rationale Becky had heard countless times from her husband. "There is nothing I can do, Mom. I have to spend the next couple of hours reviewing this proposal. It would be irresponsible as the CEO not to take care of this urgent matter now. We have over 200 employees. They depend on me to make sound judgments for our company that provides for them and their families. I also have the board meeting in January with my performance evaluation and review."

Becky stopped Ryan's explanation litany by holding her hand up in a pause measure. "Sometimes, Ryan," she interrupted, something she rarely did, "you have to make the right people, the right priority, so the right relationships are right – when and where you need them."

Ryan hung his head dejected and angry, mostly at himself, but astounded with his mother's wisdom as she walked away down the hallway. He imagined his father had heard a similar refrain from his mother. She was right, and he knew it. But he also had agreed to confirm the proposal review and needed to follow through on it. He sighed. He stood up to pace some more and at 1:55, he dialed Heather's number. She picked up after the first ring.

"Are you almost here, Ryan?" Heather asked excitedly.

Ryan was silent for just a moment, but a second was all Heather needed to interpret the likely reason for the phone call.

"Don't tell me you're not coming, Ryan!" Heather challenged with a much different tone than the one four seconds earlier. "Ryan?"

Ryan swallowed hard before admitting the truth. "I can't make it to practice, Heather. He gave her the 10-second version of the business plan and proposal he had to review, but Heather didn't really care about his CEO issues and told him so.

"Ryan, it's one thing to disappoint me, though I'm used to this in our relationship and have been for a very long time now, but it's a completely different disappointment when you break the heart of a five year old. Do you know he has been talking about this all day? Do you know how sad this is going to make him? Do you understand how much pain he has endured the past few years?"

Ryan didn't offer any additional excuses or justifications. He just said, "Please know I am really sorry and please tell Henry I am really sorry. I will make it tonight. And if you guys are still willing to enter the competition with me, I'll be there." Ryan hoped the possibility of still competing would soften the broken commitment.

"I don't know Ryan," Heather said seriously and then was silent for a few seconds. Ryan did not fill the void in communication. Heather continued, "If there is any chance of your not making it tonight – and I mean any chance, Ryan – then I am going to have to say no. So, tell me now, and understand the significance of this commitment, whether you will make it tonight. I can't promise Henry you are coming unless you are 100% sure you will be there. 6:00 at North Pole. No cell phone out. No business proposal in the car. No halfhearted effort so you can quickly get back home." Heather started to calm down and realized she was being pretty hard on Ryan, but she also realized he needed to understand this situation immediately. Heather was not a single woman. She was a single mother, a big difference. And if she was going to consider allowing Ryan in her life again – and especially in Henry's life – then Ryan would have to become a new man very, very quickly.

"If you need an hour to decide, that's fine," Heather concluded in a much calmer tone than when she had started.

"Thanks," Ryan said meekly. "I'll text you at 3:00 and let you know for sure. I will work extremely hard to get this done. I really want to see you guys and be in the contest with you."

"OK," Heather said peacefully now. "We want to see you also."

That small concession was all Ryan needed to hear. He knew he would finish the review on time. He had two hours to get it done. He'd done similar work in the same timeframe on planes, on trains, and in limousines, and he was extremely motivated to do so.

Ryan hustled through his work and texted Heather at 3:00, telling her he was almost done and would pick them up at 5:30. He flew through the business plan with his customary notes, edits, and addendums and was done by 4:00. He sent it to Tammy who forwarded it to MII's CEO. Tammy reported via text at 4:15, "All good!" Ryan was relieved, but frustrated. His work, though exhilarating and extremely profitable, was distracting him from the pursuit of Heather . . . again.

Ryan decided to walk and talk with Buford and headed out into the backyard. It was a beautiful afternoon, and he wanted some time to think. He was falling for Heather again fast, but the same issue was staring back at him. He began a conversation with his dog. "Buford, what am I doing? Heather's not going to leave Sugar Grove and North Pole. And am I ready to be a husband and a dad?" Buford responded affirmatively with a series of barks and then chased a bunny that dared to cross their path. "I don't know, boy," Ryan continued. "Maybe I need to be careful with my heart – and, more importantly, careful with

Heather's and Henry's hearts." Buford wagged his tail and, now off his leash, started to sprint toward the lake.

****

While Ryan and Buford talked through Ryan's relational concerns, Heather was doing the same thing with Jennifer, though Jennifer usually had more to say than Buford. Heather called Jennifer right after she had hung up with Ryan. Very upset Ryan had canceled, she asked Jennifer to come over with Gabby, who was already out of school, to help her settle down. Jennifer and Gabby were there in 10 minutes and the kids ironically played their new Nintendo Switches Ryan had given them, which allowed the ladies to chat.

"He is not going to leave his job, Jennifer," Heather said sadly as soon as the best friends had their coffees in their mugs and were sitting opposite each other on the couch. "We've been through this before. I am not leaving Sugar Grove and Ryan is not leaving the Twin Cities. Why even bother starting something again?

And could I be in a relationship with someone who chooses work over me, over Henry?"

Jennifer couldn't help but smile at her normally composed and contained soul sister. "First of all, Heather," Jennifer gently scolded, "you are thinking of reasons to end the relationship before it has even started, after just two days of seeing each other again! Secondly, who says one or both of you wouldn't be willing to move or change jobs if the relationship was great and headed to marriage this time? You are both in totally different stages of life now. You're over 30 and you're both executives. Wouldn't it be worth it to leave Sugar Grove and North Pole if you found your forever love? And don't you think Ryan would consider the same thing and leave the Twin Cities? Hasn't he acted very differently, very quickly this week?"

"I don't know, Jen. I have baggage this time. I loved another man. I have a child," Heather said, dejected. "Ryan is simple and yet complicated. I don't think he'll want to mess with all this," she said as she waved her arms around herself and toward Henry and Gabby.

"You were younger then. Neither of you were established in your careers. Those things matter," Jennifer exclaimed. "I know my brother and I know you. You're each very different, but you're great together. It sounds corny, but you complement each other well. Tell Ryan how you feel and what your heart wants – and, more importantly, what is required from him if you are to give him another chance. Let him process the commitment. He is different now. He is ready for change. We all see it. And I think dad's death and seeing you are the catalysts to his changed heart."

"You just want to be my sister-in-law," Heather said and gave Jennifer a big hug. "Thanks for talking with me about it. I think I would freak Ryan out, though, if I told him I still had feelings for him."

"You might," Jennifer agreed, "but you only have a few more days to decide if the risk is worth it, if Ryan is worth it. And I think he's already panicking because it's obvious he has feelings for you, too."

Chapter 7

Ryan arrived at 5:20 with, at Buford's encouragement, flowers for Heather in hand. He also had some North Pole Popcorn for both Heather and Henry. Heather was touched by the sentiment and Ryan's deeming them apology gifts. He wished he would have just been quiet about them, so Heather knew they were more than that. They jumped into Becky's Nissan Pathfinder that Heather was using while the Honda was in the shop and headed to the North Pole. Becky had already offered to give the Pathfinder to Heather, and she was thinking about accepting it, but she was having a hard time letting the Honda go.

The lot and grounds at North Pole were already full when they arrived, so they had to park in an adjacent lot. Henry was so excited he talked incessantly while holding both Ryan's and Heather's hands across the parking lots. He was so happy they were all together.

Heather checked them in, and they proceeded to their reserved space for the build. Everyone had a 20-minute time limit and had to bring their props ahead of time. Ryan's bag had a few surprises in it, which he planned to reveal only when the finishing touches were applied. Gabe, Jennifer, Tucker, and Gabby were in the space right next to them. There was friendly banter and conjecture between the siblings and their teams until the judge arrived for the rules and official start.

Jim had always taught Ryan that symmetrical snowman balls were more important than height or width. The snowman had to be pleasing to the observer and the props needed to be respectful and moderate. Ryan had each of them work on one ball. He took the largest one for the base, Heather made the second one for the middle, and Henry worked on the third one for the head. They finished their parts in about 10 minutes and Ryan modified the roundness after each ball was placed atop the other. Heather and Henry admired the precision of Ryan's work.

"Did you minor in snowmen at Powell?" Heather said playfully.

"Nope," Ryan said, "but we Millers know a thing or two about Christmas."

"This is really cool," Henry said. "I think our snowman looks awesome."

When the three balls were perfectly round and symmetrical, Ryan opened his prop bag. He gave Henry and Heather the facial elements and told them to take the lead on placing them.

"Are you sure?" Heather asked Ryan. She knew how competitive and serious he was about contests.

"Absolutely," Ryan pronounced. "We are a team!"

When the face was done, Ryan gave them a North Pole scarf and a North Pole top hat. The hat had Jim's name on the back and made Heather tear up in joyful memories. These were two items Ryan and Jim had used one of the years they won first place. Lastly, Ryan brought out an old North Pole down vest with Joe's picture dressed as Santa on the back. It was an XXXL and seemed to be made for either a plump snowman or a plump man. Ryan used giant candy canes from the North Pole gift shop for the arms and to hold up the Santa vest. Their work completed, the three of them stepped back and admired the results. Ryan glanced at his watch. They had finished with one minute to spare. It was only then that they looked over at his sister's family snowman. It was also quite cute. They had made three blocks and made a Snowman Robot with all square and rectangular pieces for the facial features, arms, and buttons down the front.

There were 20 entries and three prizes: best overall snowman, most original snowman, and most creative snowman. The most creative snowman award was first and went to a family who had made their snowman fairly skinny and dyed him with red, green, and gold. Then they had Christmas lights completely wrapped around him. It was bright, colorful, and dramatic. The next prize was the most original. Gabe and Jennifer's family won the award for their Snowman Robot they named "Frosty-Borg." Ryan, Heather, and Henry gave all their competitors high fives for their awards. The prize for best overall snowman was unanimous and went to the Miller North Pole Snowman. Heather and Ryan embraced and then brought Henry into the celebration. Everyone clapped. Jennifer later said they were clapping for Heather and Ryan's hug more than they were for their average snowman. Ryan, Heather, and Henry went forward together to receive their award, which was a giant snowman ice cream cake from the North Pole Gift Shop along with a check for $200 to go to their favorite charity. Heather and Ryan had decided on the way to the event that if they won the check, they would give it to the Sugar Grove YWCA for single mothers, so they presented the check to the director, Mary Maples, who was in attendance.

The judge thanked everyone for coming and mentioned there were free hot chocolate, ice cream sundaes, and an assortment of North Pole chocolates available in the Events Center. He also invited everyone to Tuesday night's Gingerbread House contest, for which contestants had one hour to make the best gingerbread house, and which featured the same prizes: best, most original, and most creative houses.

When Henry heard the announcement, he immediately turned to his mother and Ryan. "Can we enter that contest together, too?" He looked at Ryan first and then at his mother.

Ryan wisely waited until Heather said something. "It's OK with me if it's OK with Ryan," and she flashed Ryan such a warm and beautiful smile he would have agreed to enter any contest.

"Absolutely," Ryan said happily. "Maybe we can win again, though I admit I am not as good in the kitchen as I am in the yard."

"Then it will be my turn to lead," Heather said. "Besides, we can't be in a contest together on Wednesday because I am hosting the skating events. So, it's a good day tomorrow to see if we can win two in a row, but there are some amazing competitors in this one."

"Can we get hot chocolate now, Mom?" Henry pleaded. His desire for sugar was going to outweigh his need for contest processing. "And can we go with Gabby and Tucker?" he added.

Ryan and Heather looked over at Gabe and Jennifer, and they all agreed to walk over to the Events Center. On the way over, Gabby grabbed Ryan's hand as Heather was holding Henry's. Ryan had never felt so paternal, and he enjoyed the feeling of her little fingers in her gloves wrapped around his.

Becky appeared from out of nowhere and congratulated her children on their awards. "We'll have to save our Snowman dessert for Wednesday night after the ice skating," Becky suggested. She was always planning and organizing the family schedule and events.

"Sounds like a plan," Ryan said eagerly, and again Jennifer and Gabe looked at each other in amazement. Ryan saw their look and needled them: "Though I think the dessert is only meant for whoever wins the best overall snowman."

"Kind of played the sympathy card, though, Ryan, didn't you," Jennifer shot back, "using clothes from Grandpa and Dad? How was any judge employed by North Pole not going to vote for your North Pole Snowman?"

"You have to know the right strategies and maneuvers for victory," Ryan countered. "Wait till you see what Heather is cooking up for the gingerbread house."

Chapter 7

Heather whipped her head around to give Ryan a questioning look and then deferred to Jennifer and Becky, who were both fantastic bakers. "I am shooting for most original or most creative tomorrow," she replied. "I have no business in the same baking category as your mom and Jennifer."

"Thank you for the flattery, Heather," Becky responded. "We have Gabby on our team tomorrow also. The next great baker in the family is bringing our secret ingredient."

Ryan scooped Gabby up to tickle her and demand she reveal the secret ingredient. "I'll never tell you, Uncle Ryan," she proudly determined, "but I am glad you're home." Then she gave Ryan a bear hug around his neck and a big kiss on the cheek. "I want an ice cream sundae," she demanded as they entered the center.

"Me, too!" cried Henry.

"Me, three," added Ryan, and the four kids led the way to the dessert line. If this was what being a good uncle was all about, Ryan loved it. He hadn't felt this close to his family in a long, long time.

Becky grabbed Heather's hand as they walked behind Gabe and Jennifer, who followed the kids and Ryan. She gave her a squeeze and whispered, "You can't imagine how happy it makes me during this difficult week to have Ryan home and actually engaged with our family."

"I bet," Heather said. "I am so happy for you, the family, and for Ryan."

"I am also happy for you," Becky teased, and the two ladies gave each other shoulder hugs on their way to the hot chocolate line.

Chapter 8

Ryan woke up Tuesday contented and happy. That surprised him since this was the day of the memorial service for his father. The family kept the funeral private to not overwhelm the church. The service started at 10:00 a.m., and the open house luncheon commenced at North Pole at noon. The open house would be packed with people, and Ryan had dreaded this day for the past six months. He had known it was coming, but not knowing exactly when made it worse. Now that it was here and he was having a good time with his family and Heather, it felt like just another day, which really surprised him and made him feel guilty. It was a sad, to be sure, but he could get through it, especially because he would be with Heather for most of the day.

The service went very well. Jim was a deacon at the church and both Ryan's parents were very active there, so Pastor Steve knew them well enough to make the funeral a personal experience. Heather sat one row behind the immediate family with some of Ryan's cousins. Ryan wanted her right next to him and he almost asked her to move, but then the music started. Ryan listened to Pastor Steve talk about his father, and though nothing new was revealed, it was a great reminder of the complete life his father had lived and how his faith in God was a significant part of his purpose. Jim was a driven and strong-willed man, but one who was also compassionate, generous, and loving. The Millers had given the lead gift on the new sanctuary 15 years ago, and the dedication service was the last time Ryan had been in the building. He was pretty ashamed of it now that he was in the sanctuary again. He never found time for church in the Twin Cities, and it was another area of his life he was currently evaluating. He also knew Heather and Henry were regular attenders, and he admitted to himself that this was a part of his assessment of where church and the Lord should fit in his life.

After the service Ryan was not able to connect with Heather before she left to pick up Henry from the babysitter. He knew he would see her at the North Pole in a little bit, but he still missed engaging with her immediately after the service. Ryan reconnected with many extended family members and enjoyed the conversations more than he anticipated. *Why didn't I keep in contact with any of my family?* he thought. *Why am I so isolated from a family that wants nothing but the best for me and is a fantastic blessing?* He needed a conversation with Buford, but since Buford was back at the house, he ventured over to catch Pastor Steve before he left.

"Thanks for the service, Pastor. You really honored my dad well," Ryan shared.

"You're welcome, Ryan. Jim was a good man who loved the Lord and loved this community. But most of all, he loved your mother and his children and grandchildren." When he finished the statement, he was holding Ryan's hand and arm in a strong grip. It was obvious he wanted Ryan to understand the depth of that statement.

"I know," Ryan finally acknowledged and tried to avoid another emotional response. *What was up with these emotions?* he wondered. *They now seem to be always near the surface.* "I realized it too late to make amends, but I hope to become a better man because of it."

"I'm glad to hear that," Steve responded. "When do you want to meet for that coffee?"

"How about tomorrow morning?" Ryan asked. "I really need to talk to you about several things. I am a bit confused with my life right now."

"Does this have anything to do with Heather?" Steve probed.

"Yes, it does, Pastor," Ryan admitted. "But it's everything, really."

Chapter 8

"Alright then. How about meeting at the Grove and Grounds tomorrow at 10? How does that sound?"

"Sounds great," Ryan agreed and thanked Steve once again before he joined the rest of his family in the foyer.

****

They assumed there would be a good-sized crowd at the open house, but they were shocked when the line of cars went well out into the highway. Police officers directed traffic, and they were busy. The family processional made its way past all the cars and to their designated spots next to the Events Center. Becky had insisted the Christmas decorations stayed and the open house would be a celebration of Jim's favorite season, so there was a festive mood with Christmas music and Christmas foods. Becky worked the crowd like the First Lady of the North Pole she was, and Ryan marveled at her energy and joy. After about an hour of catching up with some old friends Ryan had forgotten he actually liked, he escaped outside and headed to the nature walk, beautifully lined with wreaths and bows. He wanted to be alone for a while and to contemplate his future. What he really needed was to cry about his dad's death, but he hadn't shed any significant tears about his father since the accident and subsequent coma happened almost seventh months ago.

Ryan spent about 30 minutes on the path, and the time alone rejuvenated him. He paused at his favorite bridge, and it was there that the tears finally came. It wasn't a weeping or a cleansing cry, but he knew it was still good that he was able to emote as he reminisced about days at the North Pole with his grandfather and father. As he came around the last corner, he heard a very familiar jingle. It wasn't Santa Claus; it was Buford's collar. Buford was running at him full speed and about knocked Ryan over in a reunion greeting. Ryan knew Buford was special, but since Buford couldn't drive, he knew someone had brought his loyal dog for him. Soon, Heather came around the same corner, smiling assuredly.

"I thought you might need your best friend for a few minutes," she said graciously. Ryan walked toward her and met her eyes. She could tell he'd been crying, so she was glad she'd asked a friend to take the hostess role an hour ago so she could pick up Buford. She hadn't dated Ryan in a long time, but she knew him well and knew what he needed when he was down – time alone and his dog. She turned around to head back to the Events Center even though she wanted to give Ryan a huge hug. Her heart ached for him, and she wanted to help him grieve.

"Wait," Ryan shouted before she was too far away. He jogged over and joined her right before the parking lot, Buford happily at his side. "Please sit on the bench with me for a minute?" he asked, motioning to the closest of the strategically placed park benches.

"OK," Heather said. Ryan took off his winter coat and wrapped it around her as they sat on the bench that overlooked the backside of the factory and the athletic fields.

"Thanks a lot, Heather," Ryan said warmly. "This means a ton to me."

"You're welcome," Heather said sincerely. "I knew Buford would help you recuperate from all the people. There are so many of our friends excited to see you. I hope it hasn't been all drudgery."

"Bringing Buford was awesome, but I mean thanks for always being kind to me even when I haven't been kind to you," Ryan stated emphatically. "You know me better than anybody other than my mother, and yet you still see the best in me. I don't deserve your friendship. I haven't earned it." Ryan was emptying part of his heart now, and though it was a bit awkward and a little over the top, Heather knew he needed to release his soul, so she let him keep going.

Chapter 8

"I have really loved seeing you and being with you these last couple of days," Ryan disclosed unabashedly. "It feels like old times, but even better."

"It has been fun, Ryan, and I look forward to our second contest tonight. And thanks for being great with Henry. He really loves your attention." Heather was the one now becoming a bit emotional and was unsure how to process Ryan's vulnerability.

"He's a great kid, Heather. You've done an amazing job raising him, especially considering everything you've been through," Ryan compassionately encouraged her.

"Thanks," Heather affirmed. "It hasn't been easy. And we still don't know why Josh gave up on us, but the last couple of years before he left something was seriously wrong with him, but he wouldn't tell me. He pulled away emotionally and mentally, and eventually he just left us and never came back. I finally filed for divorce, and he didn't even appear in court. He just had a lawyer handle everything, and they wouldn't tell me where he was. The first six months after the divorce were the toughest time of my life. I blamed myself and lost my joy and my love for people. If it hadn't been for my responsibilities with Henry and the conversations with your father, I might have slipped into a deep, deep depression."

Ryan stayed quiet and listened intently. Heather continued, "One day at work, your father pulled me aside and told me very assertively and with great conviction that I had to forgive, heal, and move on – and I couldn't wallow in my pain any longer. He told me I wasn't honoring God, Henry, or the North Pole to mope around like I was already dead." Heather was now the one to unload her soul.

"Wow," Ryan stammered. "That was a bit direct and harsh. I'm sorry my dad wasn't always very sensitive and could be tough on people."

Chapter 8

"It was tough, but it was tough love," Heather said, "and it was exactly what I needed to hear. I knew Jim cared about me, so I wasn't offended. Your dad was a really wise man, Ryan. People asked him about their personal lives as much as they asked his opinions about business and candy."

"I know," Ryan said, "and the one who probably needed his wisdom the most," pointing to himself, "was too proud to humble himself and reconcile the relationship. How stupid was I?"

"Well," Heather proclaimed, "pretty stupid," and they both laughed. "But in the spirit of your father, you need to forgive, heal, and move on. And I am talking about yourself, Ryan. You need to forgive yourself, not just your dad."

Heather had nuzzled into Ryan's side as they talked to stay warm. He turned to look at her directly as he took in the wisdom of his father through the woman who had inspired both men to love her. Ryan put his left arm around her and placed his right hand over her gloved hands. Heather's heart was beating fast. *Was this really happening today? Outside in the cold? The day of his father's funeral?*

"I would like to see you more this week, Heather," Ryan said boldly. "I really like who I am when I'm around you. I'm a better person. I'm happier and have more purpose. But it's not just about me. I love being around you."

"I would like to see you also, Ryan," Heather replied, and then she paused for several seconds before she added, "but I can't do this if this . . . us . . . is only for the week. My heart is already wide open again and so is Henry's. I don't mean to put pressure on you, but we have to keep this platonic if you aren't able to commit to me, and us, in a relationship."

Ryan was quiet, but he didn't try to escape in fear or anxiety. He stared intently at her. "The biggest mistake of my life was watching you walk away seven years ago and not doing a thing about it," Ryan confessed. "I can't do that again."

"I am not going anywhere, Ryan," Heather replied. "It's your life that is somewhere else, not mine." She said this a little more pointedly than she had intended.

"I know," Ryan said. "I am thinking through that, but right now I can't imagine being apart from you anymore." Ryan tilted his head down to hers. "Would it be OK If I kiss you?"

Heather gazed into his eyes and wanted nothing more than to kiss him, but she knew it wasn't right, at least not yet. "I really want you to, Ryan, but I don't think it's wise." And with that boundary stated, she knew she needed space. Heather moved over, took off Ryan's coat from around her shoulders, and stood up. "You didn't answer me about the relationship, Ryan." Heather said in matter-of-fact fashion. "Last time this happened, it wasn't good."

"I want a relationship, Heather. I just need a few days to get this all figured out."

"Well," Heather said passionately, "figure it out quickly, please. You are only here a few more days."

"I will," Ryan said. "Thanks again for bringing Buford. I am going to run him home. I'll be back in 30 minutes. I also need a few hours to research gingerbread houses before tonight. The contest is coming up shortly." He looked at his phone. It was a little after 2:00 p.m.

"You better," Heather laughed. "I honestly don't know what we'll make yet."

"We'll figure it out. It's just for fun tonight," Ryan said with a big smile.

The two friends walked back toward the Events Center, and Ryan instinctively reached for Heather's hand. Heather allowed her hand to grab his, but only for about two seconds. She knew if they held hands into the Events Center it would be the talk of the town, and she wasn't quite ready for that. They reached the door and Ryan gave her a quick hug and said he would see her later. He turned to Buford, "Let's go home, boy," and they turned and headed back to Ryan's car.

****

Heather was only a few feet into the Events Center when Jennifer pranced up to her with an enormous smile. "What were you and Ryan doing outside for so long?" she asked playfully.

"We were just talking," Heather answered, as seriously as she could without her inner joy spilling out into the public.

"Did you get cold and share a blanket?" Jennifer continued.

"We shared his coat and a little conversation on the bench," Heather confessed. Then she leaned forward in a whisper. "He tried to kiss me."

"What?" Jennifer squealed as quietly as she could. "But you didn't let him?"

"Nope," Heather stated. "I told him, 'Not without a commitment to the relationship.'"

"Wow, you are so mature and strong," Jennifer said. "I don't think I could have been that strong."

"I didn't say it was easy, and if I didn't have Henry, we'd still be out on the bench kissing." Heather smiled, and they both laughed and headed back to the kitchen to help Becky refill the plates and trays. The open house was still really busy and certainly doubled as a Christmas party, just as Becky had intended and Jim would have wanted.

****

Ryan was pensive and reflective on the way home and was so deep in thought he almost drove right past the turn into his parents' home. *How could I miss the most decorated driveway in Sugar Grove?* he thought as he pulled in the driveway. He decided to take Buford for a walk since he didn't get much of one at the factory. Buford obviously had the same thought and tugged on his leash to head toward the barn. "Alright, buddy," Ryan affirmed. "Let's take a lap around the property." Buford barked in agreement.

Ryan decided to peek in the barn before they went around it and was shocked at how beautiful it looked inside. It was set up for a wedding on Sunday the 26th. Jennifer had outdone herself, and Ryan made a mental note to compliment her later. He shut the door and disappeared with Buford onto the path around the timber line.

Twenty minutes later they entered the house through the back deck entrance, and Ryan went upstairs to change clothes. He opened his laptop and, tempted to look at his emails, stopped and Googled gingerbread houses instead. "Never thought I would be Googling gingerbread houses, boy," Ryan commented to Buford, who had curled up in his bed. "It's funny what you'll do when you are in love," he continued, taken aback by his own declaration. "Maybe I should tell her how I feel?"

he inquired of his loyal companion. Buford snorted in affirmation but had a hard time keeping his eyes open. "Comfortable Emoting Openly," Ryan said to Buford and laughed at the new CEO title he entered into his spreadsheet.

Ryan changed into appropriate attire for the gingerbread contest, actually looking forward to the festive environment again. He was especially relieved the funeral was over, though he knew the grieving process was a long way from over. He had to go through a ton of his dad's files, both in his filing cabinets and on his computer. His mom had asked him to do that sometime this week before he left. He splashed on some fresh cologne and scampered down the stairs and out the door. The Scrooge who normally dreaded all things Christmas whistled "Jingle Bells" on his way to his car. On the drive back to North Pole he started to envision living back in Sugar Grove. If that were the only way to be with Heather, then he was prepared to figure it out. *Maybe the Emerging board would allow me to work three days in Sugar Grove and two in the Twin Cities? Maybe they could open a second office in Sugar Grove?* His wheels turned as fast as the tires on his Corvette. He wished Buford was with him so he could bounce some things off him.

Chapter 9

When Ryan returned to the Events Center, the crowd had dwindled and the transformation from an open house to a gingerbread contest was underway. He meandered through the maze of people and took some plates and trays back to the kitchen, where a host of volunteers worked like Santa's elves. The hustle and bustle of the environment brought back fond memories of the days when he followed Grandpa Joe around the factory. Grandpa loved the busyness and festivities of the season, and Ryan used to also. He said thanks to many of his parents' friends who had made the day a big success, and, of course, many of them asked if he were coming home to run North Pole. They couldn't help themselves. Ryan left that question open-ended so as not to offend. His normal response was "We'll see."

After scanning the area thoroughly for Heather, Ryan first called and then texted her to see where she was. When she didn't answer either one, Ryan stood in the middle of the Events Center and contemplated what to do. He didn't have a Plan B for the two hours before the gingerbread contest started. He must have looked a little lost and confused because his mother finally came over to him and told him what he needed to know.

"Heather had to run home, and she never talks or texts when she drives, so don't worry. She'll be back in time for the contest," Becky assured him.

"Was it that obvious I was looking for her?" Ryan inquired.

"Well, it was to me, Honey." Becky smiled and gave her son a rub on the back. "You two really are a lovely couple. I hope you strongly consider telling her how you feel – how you have always felt about her – and soon." Becky turned to head back to the kitchen. She loved to drop truth bombs on him. She always had.

"I am, Mom," Ryan affirmed, loudly enough that she turned with a big smile and placed her hand on her heart before turning back around and disappearing through the swinging doors.

****

After they arrived home Heather knew she had to broach the subject of her potential relationship with Ryan to Henry. He wasn't old enough to have a vote or retain power in the decision, but he was certainly old enough to know and needed to be able to ask some questions. Heather knew Henry was very perceptive, so she wanted to see what his immediate thoughts and feelings were to the idea.

"Henry, we have about an hour and a half until we go back to the Center for the contest. You can have a half hour on the Nintendo after you change clothes, brush your teeth, and meet me in the living room for a five-minute talk."

"OK, Mom," Henry responded, positively. He really was a nice, obedient, respectful boy. She was so proud of him, especially considering the difficult two years he'd just been through.

About two minutes later Henry jumped onto the couch next to Heather and gave her a big hug. "Are we going to win again tonight?" Henry asked boldly.

"First of all, Henry," Heather began, "there is no way you brushed your teeth in that timeframe. Let me smell your breath."

Henry leaned over and breathed a huge breath on Heather. It actually did smell like Crest, so other than the fact Heather knew he had only brushed for maybe five seconds, she let the matter go.

"Secondly, I don't think so, Henry, but we will try our best. I am not a great baker, and there are some amazing bakers in this town, many of whom work at the North Pole and make all those cookies you love."

"Oh, I understand. They are like professional bakers."

"That's right, Honey." Then Heather turned to the topic at hand. "Henry, do you remember that Ryan is Gabby's uncle?"

"Yep. I like him. He gave me the Switch."

"That's right," Heather responded. "Before I met your father, a long time ago, Ryan and I dated for almost two years. Do you know what dating is?"

"It means you guys like each other and want to spend a lot of time together?" Henry posed, with only a fair amount of certainty.

"That's right. Where did you learn that? You are such a smart young man."

"Gabby told me about dating," Henry explained.

Heather moved on, but she'd call Jennifer later today to inform her about Gabby's four-year-old knowledge of dating. "Well, now that I am no longer married to your father and Ryan does not have a wife or a girlfriend, we are talking about maybe dating again. What do you think about that?"

"That's awesome, Mom!" Henry exclaimed. "That means me and Gabby could be related."

Heather smiled. "If we dated, it wouldn't mean we automatically would get married, and we would have to actually be married for you and Gabby to be cousins." She paused as he nodded his head. "But I wanted to make sure I talked to you about it before we decided to date."

"Great. Why don't you start dating tonight and get married this week?" Henry proclaimed. "Can I go play Switch now?"

Heather decided to let the discussion end with this humorous possibility and not explain to Henry about timeframes involved with engagements and weddings. "Absolutely," Heather declared. Henry jumped off the couch and went to retrieve the Nintendo, which was plugged in the charger. He curled up in his favorite chair, and Heather knew she had 30 minutes to herself. She pulled out her phone and saw Ryan had called and texted. She texted him back, "I'll be back to the Center around 5:30. Please don't get angry if we don't win." Then she called Jennifer to tell her the news about Gabby's relationship knowledge, and, of course, about possibly dating Ryan.

****

The three snowman champions were positioned at a corner table, where, they all acknowledged, they belonged. They did not have the front tables that were reserved for the professional bakers, so the crowd could see their works of art as they developed. The front tables, however, did include Becky, Jennifer, and Gabby, and Becky planned to recreate the factory gingerbread house she was then using as a Christmas centerpiece.

The rules of the contest were simple. Each team had one hour to build a gingerbread house using only the materials provided. The house had to be able to stand on its own and would be judged by some of the ladies of the North Pole that had won many of the gingerbread contests in the past. There was a much more serious atmosphere for this contest than was present with the snowman affair, and Ryan could tell Heather was nervous.

"Hey, team," Ryan whispered to Heather and Henry, "let's build something unique and different. We didn't have time to practice, so we should try and win the most creative house. What do you guys think?"

"Sounds great," Heather said, relieved.

"OK, great," Ryan responded. "What should we build?" He looked at Heather, but it was Henry who spoke up first.

"How about a fire station?" Henry suggested. His father Josh was a fireman, so Heather was not sure how Ryan would respond to this suggestion – or if he even knew that fact. Ryan looked to Heather for confirmation, and she gave with a smile and a head nod.

Chapter 9

"Firehouse it is," Ryan pronounced.

The firehouse was pretty decent by the time it was done. It featured two stories and was modeled after Sugar Grove's fire station. The strongest element of their house was the large candy cane – minus the cut-off curve for the two-story fireman pole. When Heather and Ryan looked around at some of the other houses, they knew they would not win any of the three prizes. As the judges moved around the room, Ryan noticed Heather had some gingerbread stuck in her hair. He gently removed it and brushed her cheek with his hand at the same time, something that wasn't necessary to remove the particles of bread. She smiled but tilted her head and looked at Henry, who was watching, so Ryan intuited he should not continue.

Becky, Jennifer, and Gabby won the best gingerbread house, a truly stunning replica of the original factory. The other two awards went to other ladies, who like Becky, had been honing their gingerbread skills for decades. Ryan, Heather, and Henry left their table to join the victors, and Becky invited them all to come back to her house to celebrate. Ryan looked at Heather hopefully and Henry was already begging. "Please, Mom, please. Can we?"

"OK," Heather relented, "but we can only stay for a little while. It's been a long day already." Henry barely let Heather finish her approval before he interjected and informed the family about a major development.

"My mom and Ryan are dating now," Henry proudly exclaimed to punctuate the moment. Everyone stopped their preparation for departure and stared at the now blushing Ryan and Heather. Henry continued. "They started dating today and might get married this week." Now there was extreme surprise on all the faces.

Ryan was as shocked as everyone else, but he also felt a surge of adrenaline and wasn't the least bit embarrassed by Henry's declaration. Heather, on the other hand, was mortified and put her hands over her mouth, but the rest of the family was so obviously happy about the news she didn't offer any counter information.

No one spoke or altered the air of anticipation for the next 30 seconds as they headed toward the exit doors. Finally, Heather shared, "Everybody can stop staring at me. I'll explain later. Henry, let's get to the car and head over to Grandma Becky's right away."

But Henry was not done with the disclosure and was confused by his mother's lack of affirmation of the news he had shared. He let go of her hand and turned to face the Millers. "But Mom, you told me you might start dating or get married," Henry continued. "You said, 'Absolutely.'"

Heather, normally full of social graces and easy in conversation, abruptly stopped walking and froze in a paralyzed moment of shock. Everyone else paused, too, enveloped in a thunderous moment of absolute silence. Heather had no idea what to say, so Ryan bailed her out.

"Henry, thanks for sharing with us. I am absolutely looking forward to dating your mother."

"OK," Henry said, satisfied. "Can we go to Grandma Becky's now?" and everyone recommitted to the walk to the cars.

Ryan, however, decided to take advantage of Heather's rare awkwardness and played off her embarrassment for an assertive move with the family. "Well, since Heather and I are now dating, we'll leave her car here and she can ride home with me in the Corvette. Henry, if your mother is cool with this, you can go with Gabby and Tucker."

"Awesome," Henry shouted, and Gabby squealed in delight, after Heather confirmed the transportation arrangements with a head nod. Heather was too shocked and embarrassed to offer any verbal rebuttal or different arrangement. She grabbed Ryan's hand and pulled him in the direction of his car without even looking at the rest of the family, including Henry. "We'll see you guys there," she shouted over her shoulder.

"Can't wait to hear all about this!" Jennifer yelled across the lot.

****

Heather apologized as soon as they were safely in his car. "I'm sorry about the dating thing, Ryan. I had to talk to Henry about the possibility before I told you how I felt, and I forgot to tell him not to talk about it. He misunderstood my 'absolutely' comment. I had said 'absolutely' to affirm his desire to play Nintendo, not to affirm we would start dating today, and certainly not to affirm getting married this week." She was flustered, and Ryan enjoyed seeing her this way. Both of them were relieved the topic was now open for discussion.

"No apology needed," Ryan replied. "I am glad Henry brought it up, and I am glad you talked to him about it because I know you wouldn't have if you didn't feel about me the same way I feel about you." Ryan smiled broadly and squeezed her hand as he finished the sentence, and they turned onto the highway.

Ryan wasn't finished sharing yet and let seven years of pent-up emotions erupt from his heart as he stared at the windshield and the open road ahead of them. "Heather, I love you and always have. I let you walk away seven years ago, which was the dumbest move of my life – even dumber than not talking to my dad. I was proud, stubborn, arrogant, and childish, and I have been alone ever since. I am so sorry that Josh left you and divorced you, and I don't know how a man could do that to the two of you, but for me it is another chance, and I am prepared to do whatever is necessary, including leaving the Twin Cities and leaving my job, to be in a relationship with you again." The speech came across authentic, sincere, and heartfelt. It should have because Ryan had rehearsed it several times with Buford, who seemed to be moved by it every time.

Heather sat quietly, so stunned she didn't know what to say. Her heart wanted to explode with excitement, but she didn't want to respond too quickly. She didn't think Ryan would start this deeply, and she also knew there was likely more coming from him if she didn't fill the silence. Twenty seconds later Ryan confirmed her suspicion.

"I understand if you are not able to respond to this right now, but I want to say something else extremely important," Ryan continued, quite emboldened with passion. "I am also prepared to be involved in Henry's life – and I mean permanently. Even if we don't date or get married, I am prepared to be a father figure for him, if that is something you are OK with, but, if not, at least an uncle figure. He needs men in his life, and I already remind him of my father. I won't try to replace Josh, but I want to be a positive, male influence in his life. He is a really awesome young man." Ryan paused and looked at Heather, who had begun to cry softly into her scarf. He was happy she was emotional but then began to doubt whether this was a positive response or not as her silence continued.

"Oh no," Ryan said under his breath, more to himself than to her. "I've said too much, haven't I? I'm really sorry. I just don't want to let another day or another hour pass without telling you how I feel about you and Henry."

Heather was too overwhelmed to say something trite or random, so she took another minute or two to compose herself. Inside, Ryan was panicking, but he thought he should shut up for a while and not have any more streams of consciousness or releases of repressed feelings. He needed to hear from Heather's heart, and she normally was not the inhibited one. They were about a mile from Becky's house when Heather finally responded.

"Please don't go to your house yet, Ryan," Heather suggested. "We need to talk some more before we are with the whole family."

"You're right," Ryan said. "I know Jennifer can't wait to drill us about this. I'll be glad to keep driving, and I really need to hear how you feel about what I have shared. But would you text Mom quickly and tell her we'll be there in 20 minutes, so she doesn't worry."

"Of course," Heather said, texting Becky the news. Becky read the text out loud to the family, prompting *oohs* and *aahs* of speculation.

They passed the house and as soon as they were back on the main road through town, the freedom to have more time was all Heather needed. "Ryan, I love you also and always have," Heather said passionately but without looking at Ryan. "But I appropriately turned that love off for the past seven years, and it has come back so strongly and so quickly that I am struggling to know what to do about it." This time it was Ryan who wisely stayed silent. After about ten more seconds, Heather continued.

"And Henry is a part of this equation. No man can love me without loving him, so I am glad you declared your intentions toward him as part of your disclosure, and I know you mean it. Tonight, you took away the one barrier I thought would always exist, which has always kept my love from being fully released to you. I can't believe you are willing to leave the Twin Cities and your job for us! That's almost more than I can take at the moment." Heather again began to cry, this time pretty strongly.

Ryan had tears stream down his own face, and he let the moment soak in as they drove through downtown Sugar Grove. He was proud of himself for sharing his heart and also amazed, as usual, with

Heather's heart. Heather saw the tears on Ryan's face and was startled with this new side of Ryan, so she waited for Ryan to speak next. Ryan, sensing her desire, decided to lighten the mood a little bit.

"Well, girlfriend," Ryan said flirtatiously, "I think if we are going to do this, we need to do it right. Why don't we go back to the house and tell the family that Henry was right? We are dating again, discussing the possibilities for the future, and would appreciate if we were given some space and time to work through the details. It is, after all, still the day that we buried my father."

"Sounds really smart," Heather affirmed. "All of it sounds good. I can't believe we are dating again!" She pleasantly laughed a little bit in disbelief and reached for his hand. "Wait till the town hears about it and, man, your dad would be so happy." With that recognition, tears flowed freely and unashamedly in the Corvette.

"I know," Ryan said, taking her hand and putting it on her leg. "This news is probably the only thing in the world that makes this day actually positive for my mother. And yes, this news will be the talk of Christmas in Sugar Grove; it is kind of like our family to dominate the Christmas spirit in this town. I look forward to sealing this new dating status with a kiss, but I don't want it to be in the car." Ryan looked at Heather to see if he had any chance of a kiss before they went back to his mom's. He didn't have to wait long.

"Well," Heather said with a huge grin, "let's pull over by the park and walk out to the gazebo as we used to."

"Best idea all night," Ryan agreed, pulling the Corvette over immediately, parking abruptly, and turning the engine off quickly. He stumbled out of the front seat, slipped on the ice, and fell flat on his back. He wasn't hurt and told Heather that, but they both enjoyed a good laugh. Heather started to step out of the car, but Ryan barked at her to wait as he slid around to her side of the car.

"Smooth," Heather laughed while placing her hand out for assistance.

"I know," Ryan said, laughing at himself, "as always. I've waited seven years to get a chance to kiss you again, so forgive me for a little nervous energy."

"Forgiven now and forgiven for the past," Heather replied seriously, giving Ryan a big hug after he shut the door. The two then walked slowly, hand and hand, to the gazebo. Ryan led her to the middle of the floor. As this was not the first time they had been to the gazebo for a romantic interlude, they both found their initials in the benches littered with engravings from couples. Instead of immediately kissing her, Ryan pulled out his phone. Heather, dumbfounded, didn't know what to say.

Ryan knew she would be confused, so he put his right hand up in a wait motion and then pulled up his playlist. He turned the volume up on his phone and played "Last Christmas" by Wham, Heather's favorite Christmas song. "May I have this dance?" Ryan asked as he bowed and placed his hand forward and took Heather's hand.

"Absolutely," Heather gushed with pleasure, relieved Ryan had not intended to check his emails or texts. He grabbed her hand and pulled her into his arms. In reference to the song, Ryan echoed George Michael's chorus, though he spoke it rather than sang it. "I gave your heart away, and I won't do it again," and with that sentiment he leaned in and kissed her twice softly on the cheek before meeting her lips.

They danced slowly and rhythmically and didn't talk at all. When the song finished, Ryan gave her another kiss and then led her back toward the car. "Let's go share the news with Mom and the family. I am sure they are anxiously awaiting us."

"For sure," Heather agreed. "I'll text Becky and tell them we are on the way."

The two talked freely and easily on the drive back to Becky's, the pressure of the potential relationship having been resolved – they were officially dating again. Now, old friends caught up on some of what they missed over the past seven years within the autonomy of a renewed commitment. They arrived at the house and scampered up the sidewalk, prepared to greet the peanut gallery, but there was no one in the hallway, kitchen, or the great room except Buford, who seemed confused also. Heather called out to Henry, and Ryan called out to Gabby, and after a few seconds, they finally heard some giggles from the basement.

The happy couple went down the stairs and, turning the corner to the entertainment area, were met with "SURPRISE!" There were streamers and balloons and a sign that Tucker made that said, "Happy Dating." Heather and Ryan burst out laughing, and all the family engulfed them with hugs and congratulations. What a crazy day this had been for Ryan. A memorial service for his father. The Christmas-themed open house. The gingerbread contest. The slip-up by Henry about dating that led to the kiss and the commitment to Heather. "Crazy Enlightened Outcome," Ryan muttered to himself and into his phone app. Buford barked in agreement.

Chapter 10

Wednesday morning Ryan walked into the Grove and Grounds at 9:55, and Pastor Steve, who had strategically picked that location so Ryan would not be intimidated by the intimacy of face-to-face interaction, was already there at the counter. They had had several awkward and uneventful one-on-one meetings in the past, but this time Ryan sat down quickly, ordered his drink, and started to share before Steve even asked him a question or said hello.

"We kissed last night, Pastor, and we are officially dating again," Ryan declared confidently, almost out of breath in his excitement to share the news. He had prepared his opening statement on the way to the shop.

"Wow," Steve responded, truly surprised. He had counseled Heather before and after the divorce and did not anticipate her dating again this soon, especially with Ryan. Ryan was one of several men in her life who had abandoned her. She had a pretty strong father wound that had been carried out with Ryan and Josh, among others.

Ryan continued, "Heather talked to Henry about the possibility of our dating, and Henry spilled the beans to the whole family after the gingerbread contest. So, on the way back to our house, Heather and I talked about it and decided to give it a go." Ryan was amped up, and he hadn't even had caffeine yet. Pastor Steve had never seen Ryan like this before and was a bit startled by his new demeanor. This was not the typical follow-up coffee with a man who had buried his father the day before. This certainly wasn't going to be the typical coffee talk with Ryan, either.

"Congratulations," Steve said, genuinely happy for him. "I guess then the major question for us to talk about this morning is how you will manage a long-distance relationship. From what I remember in the past, that didn't work too well for you guys the first time."

"You're right, Pastor," Ryan admitted, "but I am prepared to leave the Twin Cities and move back to Sugar Grove." Ryan was so direct and sure about himself and his future that Steve took much longer to respond than the comment seemed to warrant.

"I am thrilled for you, Ryan, but I am also quite surprised. Have you talked to your Board about this yet?" Steve wondered whether Ryan had really thought this through.

"No, I haven't," Ryan answered, "but I am prepared to present the Board with some options for splitting my time between the Twin Cities and Sugar Grove at our January board meeting. And honestly, Steve, I am prepared to resign if I need to. I am sick of being alone. I am tired of being away from my family. I have all the money and things I want, and I haven't been happy in years." Ryan's coffee was placed next to him, and he took a couple of quick sips. Steve hoped the coffee served as a sedative.

Ryan continued unabated. "When I am with Heather, I am the kind of man I want to be, the kind of man that my dad would have been proud of." Both men sat silently for a minute, and Pastor Steve took a moment to absorb the burgeoning soul of the previously bound-up man.

"This is quite a turn of events, Ryan," Steve finally acknowledged. "I have to ask the obvious question, then, in response to this line of thinking and the obvious transformational change of heart taking place. If Emerging says no, what are you going to do?"

Ryan sat stoically for at least a minute and then surprised Steve again. "Until this morning, I would have told you, 'I have no idea.' But after yesterday, being at the Events Center, mingling with the people who love my family, walking around the factory the past three days, recognizing my stupidity about my father, spending time with my sister and her family, and starting to date Heather and be involved with Henry, I woke up this morning and said, 'Why not? Why not be the CEO at North Pole!'"

Steve turned to face Ryan more directly, no longer as worried about the intimacy factor as he had been five minutes earlier. "I am so happy to hear all this, Ryan. And frankly, I have known you for 15 years and never seen you this outward and happy – especially given that you just buried your father yesterday. You seem to be open now to everything – change, humility, relationship, and love. I am seriously impressed. It takes a man of integrity and courage to consider these kinds of changes at this stage of life and to act upon them quickly."

"Thanks," Ryan said warmly. "It means a lot to me to hear you say that. I trust you to tell me the truth and let me know if I am crazy or not. I really blew it with Heather last time, and I am not going to do that again. Now I need to ask you a different question. How do I forgive myself for not reconciling with my father?"

Steve took a minute, several sips of his coffee, and a bite of his donut, and then communicated what he hadn't expected to get to this morning. "Ryan, let me answer the question by sharing a story about your father." He paused for effect, and it worked. Ryan leaned in, rapt with attention. Steve continued emphatically, "Your dad specifically asked me to tell you this story sometime after he died. You know your, dad, Ryan; he always thought and planned ahead."

Ryan put his coffee down and turned completely to face Steve – a bit odd of an odd look, two men so intimately in focus at the restaurant counter. Ryan had not expected this and was excited to hear a message from his father. "That would be great," Ryan said. "Please share."

Chapter 10

"Before your father took over as CEO at North Pole, he and your grandfather had a big dispute about the future of the company. Jim wanted to expand, franchise little North Pole shops throughout Minnesota, and narrow the focus of production. He wanted to eliminate more than half of the candy and only sell the lines with huge profit margins. Makes business sense, right?"

Steve paused again to allow Ryan to nod in affirmation before continuing.

"Jim put together an elaborate business plan with projected revenue changes that would have doubled, if not tripled the annual net income for the company. He was already COO, so it wasn't as if he didn't have factual experience and evidence for this proposal. Joe listened carefully to his oldest son and told Jim he needed a few days to digest the information, pray about it, and consult with the Board."

Ryan interrupted for a second when Steve stopped to take another drink. "Do you know what year this happened?"

"I am not exactly sure," Steve answered, "but I know you were a boy so I would imagine sometime in the early 1990's. "

"OK. I was probably in grade school. Please continue."

"Well, I don't know if you knew this Ryan, but your Grandpa Joe was not a great businessman, at least when it came to the financials. He was a visionary. A pioneer. An amazing leader of people." Steve stopped for a second to look at Ryan intently to observe his nonverbal responses to these revelations about the man he idolized his whole life.

"I don't know if I really knew that," Ryan admitted. "I just assumed he was like Dad and me."

"Nope," Steve retorted quickly. "You and Jim are natural firstborn leaders with structure, organization, and linear processing. Your grandpa was a middleborn visionary, whose love was the people, not the product or the production. According to Jim, Becky, and several others I know, Joe was smart enough to hire people around him that were excellent in areas he wasn't, and that included your dad, but Joe had amazing business instincts and knew what the culture and community needed. He always thought beyond himself and your family."

"That partly explains why Grandpa gave me the jobs he did when I worked there in the summers," Ryan said pensively.

"Exactly," Steve affirmed with a nod of his head. "Anyway, Joe really did think and pray about the opportunities that Jim presented but decided to not do any of them, at least not right away, and Jim was devastated. And really, more than devastated. He was furious, so mad, that he resigned." Steve stopped after that statement, aware that Ryan probably didn't know that bit of North Pole and Miller family history.

"What?" Ryan said incredulously and with more volume than he realized. "I never knew that. Are you sure?" Several people stopped what they were drinking or saying and glanced over at the animated conversation. "I never knew Dad to work anywhere besides North Pole – for my whole life."

"Positive," Steve said confidently. "I've seen the letter. Jim showed it to me and then gave it to me to give to you. I have it at the church. I didn't expect us to talk about North Pole today, or I would have brought it with me."

"This is amazing. I never knew Dad and Grandpa had any issues working together. They always seemed like two peas in a pod. What happened next?"

"Your grandfather wouldn't accept the resignation and made your father present it to the Board." Steve built more anticipation with the tone and tempo of the story, just like a Sunday-morning sermon. "Jim didn't work for the next few days until the Board meeting, at which time he explained the rationale for his resignation. The Board listened, asked good questions, and then, like Joe, refused to accept it." Steve paused again and looked at Ryan, who was reeled in like a largemouth bass.

"I've been with many boards," Ryan exclaimed, quite intrigued by this process. "I've never known a board to have the power or leverage to refuse a resignation. There must have been some sneaky details in his contract."

"The board didn't have that power, nor was there language in Jim's contract," Steve responded with a smile, ready to deliver the massive twist in the story. "Instead, they countered his resignation by offering him the CEO position and moved Joe to the President role. It was a better fit for the company and a much better fit for both men. Jim gladly accepted and that is when the company took off to become what it is today."

"Wow. That's really cool!" Ryan said, amazed and a bit shocked over this narrative. "But as far as I remember," Ryan stammered, "North Pole never did the initiatives Dad brought to Grandpa in the first place."

"Correct," Steve confirmed. "Jim accepted the role immediately. It included a nice raise and a new office, but it also included a year probation for major initiatives. Money was tight at that juncture, and North Pole needed to secure investors, make some major purchases in capital expenditures, and create a vision and strategic plan for the future. It was plenty of work to keep Jim motivated and moving."

"This is fascinating," Ryan declared, sitting back in his stool for the first time since the beginning of the conversation. "Thanks so much for sharing this with me. What happened after the first year?"

"I don't know," Steve said sheepishly. "He told me you would know."

"What?" Ryan said, seriously irritated. "Are you kidding me?"

"No," Steve said surprised. "I thought when I reached this part of the story you would actually be able to tell me what happened next. I want to know also."

"This is just like Dad," Ryan complained, his good mood instantly souring. "Why wouldn't he just tell you the end of the story and how this is supposed to help me?"

"I'm sorry, Ryan," Steve apologized. "I don't know what the business side of the answer is, but I think I understand the point of priority and emphasis. There must be some documents somewhere to explain the rest. I am confident if you don't know the answer that it must be available to you."

"Man, I hope you are right," Ryan said. "Otherwise, I think I am more confused about him now than I was before. Why didn't he follow through on any of those changes? North Pole has been doing business pretty much the same way for 20 years. They are doing well, but I would also want to make major changes if I took over."

"I understand," Steve said. "Maybe that is why your father wanted me to tell you the story. Maybe he knew you would be free to consider returning home once he was out of the picture. Have you looked through your dad's files or computer yet?"

"No, I haven't," Ryan admitted, "but I guarantee you I will when I get home. Do you mind if I hustle home to do that?"

"Of course not," Steve exclaimed. "Just do me one favor."

"What's that?" Ryan asked.

"Withhold judgment until you know what happened," Steve replied.

"I'll try," Ryan promised.

"And one more thing," Steve continued, "tell me when you find out. I won't be able to get it out of my mind until you let me know."

"Of course," Ryan said, giving Pastor an aggressive handshake and the waitress $20 before Steve could debate with him about who would pay. "Could we meet again before I talk to the Emerging board?" Ryan asked as he turned to leave, "and talk more about this story after I ponder it for a while?"

"Sure," Steve replied. "I look forward to it." And for the first time in the last decade, he really meant it. Conversations with Ryan used to be so serious and dour. This meeting had invigorated the pastor and also created an illustration for his Christmas sermon about new birth.

****

Ryan texted Heather a quick update before he started the car to head back home. "The talk with Pastor Steve was great," he typed, "and I learned some new things about Dad and Grandpa Joe. Please give me a call at lunch if you have time." Ryan knew she might not respond right away because she had a full workday at North Pole. Their plan was to meet at the ice rink around 5:00, so Ryan could help with the final preparations for the ice skating contest, which was Heather's contest to organize and operate. Ryan also checked in with Tammy to see how the week was unfolding for Emerging. He wanted to tell her about his ideas, but he knew it was too soon. Tammy said things were running smoothly with no issues. Ryan knew that wasn't completely true, but he was too focused on his dad to pry or provoke Tammy into the deeper matters at Emerging this week. She was a great office manager and could handle most anything that arose while he was gone. He made a mental note to give her a nice raise after the New Year.

Ryan parked in the driveway next to his father's favorite car, a white 1957 T-Bird that really should have been back in the barn or in a covered facility. He ran up the sidewalk and into the house. As his mother greeted him, he asked her to make him a quick sandwich. Sitting down at the kitchen table, he told her the whole story of his coffee meeting with Pastor Steve before challenging her with some questions he had contemplated on the way back to the house.

"Mom," Ryan started, "why didn't you or Dad ever tell me about the issues between Dad and Grandpa? I had no idea Dad had threatened to resign back in the 90's."

Becky was prepared for this conversation. She had been for years, but she was also ready because Pastor Steve called her after the breakfast chat. "Ryan, I have told you many times Dad and Grandpa didn't always get along. I even told you they had some huge disagreements. You never seemed interested in hearing more about them. For the record, your dad didn't tell me about the resignation, either, until a few years ago, and by that time you weren't really talking to us much." Becky still had some sadness in her voice due to the separation, and Ryan felt terrible hearing it. She continued, "Your father was a proud man, Ryan. He didn't tell me about many of the difficult things he went through at work. He was from a different era, Honey."

Ryan nodded in agreement, fully enjoying his mother's BLT and the new, open communication style with his loved ones. "Did you know about his big dreams for North Pole? Franchising? Streamlining product lines? Expanding the brand?" Ryan asked, hoping she knew more than Steve had.

"Not really, Honey," Becky said apologetically. "Your father might have mentioned some of those things to me, but you know I don't have a business mind. It was just marital conversation to me. He never asked my opinion about those kinds of decisions. He would ask me about the parties, the events, and the taste of the candy, things like that," she said with fond remembrance in her voice.

"Well," Ryan replied, "Pastor Steve is sure Dad left me information to fill in the gaps in the story. He said Dad specifically told him to tell me that story after he died. Why? It has to mean something significant to me, and I want to know. I'm going to spend a couple of hours in Dad's office if you don't mind. Where are his keys to the filing cabinet and his computer passwords?" he implored.

"All of the information you need is in the middle desk drawer," Becky answered. "Have fun, and please feel free to recycle or shred old documents we won't need."

"Thanks, Mom," Ryan said as he backed away from the table and stood up. "The sandwich was amazing, as always, and it really has been good to be home for a while. I haven't felt this relaxed in Sugar Grove in a long time," he admitted.

"You haven't been in love in a while, either," Becky reminded him.

"You're right, Mom. That feels really good also. Heather is amazing. Why didn't I fight for her last time?" Ryan asked, mainly to himself.

Becky answered anyway. "You weren't ready to be a husband seven years ago, Ryan. I am not trying to be mean, but you were pretty selfish and self-absorbed back then."

"I know, Mom. It's sad. I think I was that way until about a year ago, but I was still too proud to come home and really talk to Dad." Ryan was rarely publicly reflective like this, so Becky, though a bit surprised, shared more.

"Ryan, your dad loved you so much. He could be selfish and stubborn, just like you. He was a very, very smart businessman, just like you. And though you haven't asked, he left you a lot of money in his will and several of his cars. He also left you a large percentage of the North Pole. He was still the majority owner when he died, so that makes you the primary owner. Congratulations! You own a company! You own Grandpa Joe's North Pole!"

"Holy cow!" Ryan exclaimed, sitting back down as he received the news, spontaneous tears flowing freely down his cheeks. "I expected he would probably leave me some cars or some money, but not North Pole. I don't deserve it." And then it happened. The tears stored up in his soul for almost a decade began to spill. Soon they turned into sobs, and he slumped out of his chair, crumpled to the floor, and bawled.

Buford was the first comforter to approach and curled up next to his master. Ryan hugged him as his body heaved. Becky gave both of them some space for a few minutes and, after the sobs subsided, joined Ryan and Buford on the floor with a hand on both.

"Believe it or not Ryan," Becky said lovingly, "your dad always held out hope you would come back and run North Pole, even when you told him it would be the last choice you would ever make as a businessman. I don't want to heap burning coals upon your head, but you can't imagine how much that statement hurt your father's pride and his heart."

"I know, Mom. It was a stupid and selfish thing to say. I am so sorry – sorry to you, sorry to Dad, sorry to the whole family. I was ungrateful, conceited, and stubborn. When I got out of college, I felt strongly about not working at North Pole, but I could have communicated my intentions graciously and respectfully. I knew I was letting down Dad and even Grandpa, and I never really grieved or got over Grandpa's death, either. Then, I screwed up the relationship with Heather. I was a mess. All my pride and ego cost me the last years of Dad's life. Every person I've talked to since I've been home shares a story with me of what Dad did for them or meant to them, and I chose to be out of that influence and wisdom because I was immature and idiotic." Ryan gave his mother's hand a squeeze and helped her up off the floor as he rose back into his seat. "Please forgive me, Mom."

"You are forgiven, Ryan, and though you can't get that time back, you can choose very specifically what you will do with your time from this moment forward – with the family, with North Pole, and with Heather and Henry," said Becky, sliding into the chair next to Ryan.

"I think I have realized the significance of that truth since the moment I came home for the funeral and instinctively drove to North Pole first," Ryan confessed. "In driving there and then walking along the property, I recognized that home to me is not just you and Jennifer and this house. It's North Pole, too. It's as if I have returned to both of my homes."

"Your father was pretty hopeful this would happen when he was no longer in the way. He didn't necessarily mean his death, but as you know, God determines our days, not man. But he did believe you would one day come back and run the business. He truly believed it was your destiny and, more importantly, your calling from God – just as it had been for him and Grandpa Joe. Dad didn't think you would get right with him or right with North Pole until you were right with God first," Becky summarized.

Ryan received the message from his mother and the Lord and sat in contemplative silence for a minute. Finally, he looked at her with tenderness. "It's all pretty overwhelming, Mom. Does Heather know I own North Pole?" Ryan asked, not sure whether he hoped she knew or not.

"No, she doesn't, Ryan," Becky explained. "Your father and I both felt it was best she didn't know, especially as she became such an important part of the leadership team. She really is amazing in her role of VPHR. Everyone loves her."

"Not as much as I do." Ryan smiled, completely open now with his smitten heart.

Chapter 10

Returning to the task at hand, Becky said, "I am sure you will find the documents of your ownership in your father's files. And just so you know, your father left Jennifer this house and the other properties we own, which I am sure doesn't bother you a bit. I am actually trying to talk her and Gabe into moving in with me soon. I get very lonely in this big old house. Having the grandkids around would keep me young."

"I totally understand, Mom, and I'm glad Dad left Jennifer the houses. I hope they do move in with you. They could also rent or sell their current house and use the money for a college fund." Ryan was already estate-planning for his sister.

Ryan figured it was as good a time as any to share the new vision on which he had recently been ruminating. "To tell you the truth, Mom, I had been thinking about talking to some of the North Pole board members about applying for the CEO position. I am not leaving Heather again, and if Emerging is not willing to have a remote CEO, then I might not have a choice."

Becky slid off her chair and gave Ryan a big hug, and this time she wept, also releasing some pent-up grieving from the loss of her husband. Ryan held his mom and Buford put his head on her lap.

After a few minutes she continued, "That would make me the happiest woman in the world. To have my son home running the family business . . . and married to one of my favorite people, my second daughter . . . and a new grandson or two or three. Wow, what a gift from God in the midst of a very sad week. The Lord giveth and the Lord taketh away," Becky affirmed, quoting the famous recognition of God's sovereignty over life from the book of Job. "Thank you, Honey. Let me know what you find out in the office. I am heading to town to get some groceries and you need to get to work."

"OK, Mom. Thanks," Ryan said, "for everything," and Buford followed Ryan down the hall and into the office.

****

Heather saw the text from Ryan when it was delivered but couldn't respond to him until after lunch. She had been teased about Ryan mercilessly all morning by the other executives, and she thoroughly enjoyed it. Only her administrative assistant Mandy, however, received the full story – that she and Ryan were actually dating.

Heather went into her office and shut the door to call Ryan, even though the glass walls and glass door didn't exactly allow true privacy. She sat in her chair and turned to face the window that looked over the back of the North Pole property and the bench where she and Ryan had snuggled just yesterday. Ryan picked up on the first ring.

"Hey, Ryan," she said casually. How do they talk now that we are dating again after all these years? she wondered.

"Hey, Heath," Ryan responded, intentionally using his nickname for her when they previously dated.

"Wow, it's really great to hear you call me that again," Heather admitted, beaming. "Unfortunately, I only have about five minutes. Fill me in on the meeting with Pastor Steve and the news about your father."

Ryan proceeded to give her a quick recap, his initial irritation with Pastor Steve's story abated courtesy of the additional information from his mother. He told her he was about to hibernate in his dad's office for the afternoon and would see her at the ice rink as scheduled. He also asked it if were alright if Buford came and if she had any ideas on a date for him. She let him know Buford was welcome to attend, but she couldn't guarantee a date for him.

"Perhaps Buford should try an online service," she teased.

Ryan decided not to tell her about his ownership of North Pole yet. He planned to tell her that night after the event. He trusted his mom and Steve, but he thought it was wise to have the documents in hand before sharing their new reality. They were not only dating. They were also in business together. Ryan was her boss!

Heather listened intently to the story and was just as fascinated with the lack of closure as Ryan was. "Please call me and tell me what you find out," Heather asked. "Even if I can't pick up, leave me a voice mail, so I can listen at my first possible opportunity."

"Sure will," Ryan replied, ecstatic to have someone to share his life with finally. "Thanks for caring. It means a lot to me."

"You're welcome. You can tell me all about it later at the gazebo," Heather said flirtatiously.

Ryan loved the playfulness and followed suit. "Sounds like a great idea. I'll go practice getting in and out of my car."

They both laughed, and though she hated to do it, Heather hung up, so she wouldn't be late for her next meeting.

Chapter 11

It took Ryan almost an hour to find the ownership document which was signed by all the board members and a notary. It was official – he owned North Pole. He stared at the document for quite a while and suddenly became quite emotional again. He turned to Buford for a discussion. They hadn't talked in a while.

"Buford, why do I keep getting emotional about owning North Pole? My entire adult life I have tried not to run the company and now that I own it, I think I wanted to run it all along. Man, buddy, I have got to get a hold of my emotions. They are starting to appear too frequently." Ryan didn't look at Buford when he talked but continued to stare at the ownership document and scratch Buford's head. He continued, "Buford, old boy, how would you like to move back to Sugar Grove?" Ryan had rescued Buford from the Sugar Grove Shelter a year before he moved to the Twin Cities. Both of them were locals at heart.

Ryan made several piles for the important documents. He had a shredding pile, a copy pile, a save pile, and a recycle pile. His dad was meticulous with his organization, so it was not difficult for Ryan to make sense of the paperwork. The most surprising documents Ryan found were the tax returns. For the last decade his father and mother had given away over a million dollars a year to local, state, and national charities. He was stunned. He knew they were wealthy and generous, but this took it to a new level. *I am going to step up my giving, too*, he promised. He was unfamiliar, however, with one of the organizations which received a large gift each of the past two years: the Minnesota Rehabilitation Center in Evergreen Township. Looking it up on his phone, he discovered it to be a small township three and a half hours northwest from Minneapolis. He made a mental note to ask his mom about it. The Rehabilitation Center had been in existence for almost a century and handled all major addictions.

Three hours went by quickly, during which he learned a lot about the company, the properties his sister now owned, and his father. What he didn't learn, however, was anything about the disagreement between his dad and his grandfather and the subsequent change in strategic planning. He wasn't angry as much as he was disappointed, but after consulting with Buford, he decided it was enough digging for today. There were still hundreds of files to go through on the computer. He would spend more time looking sometime tomorrow.

Ryan left Heather a message about not finding a few specific answers, but still discovering some pretty important and interesting stuff. "I'm looking forward to seeing you and Henry soon," he texted. He also mentioned Buford had indeed found several dates for tonight's contest and was in consideration mode for the final selection process. When he had finished cleaning everything, he took Buford outside for a long walk, and both enjoyed the crisp and cold winter air. The winds were picking up from the west, which usually meant some more snow was on the way.

****

Ryan arrived at North Pole just before 5:00. Despite the playful banter he and Heather enjoyed about his best friend, Ryan left Buford at home. The parking lot was in transition from the factory workers to the contest participants, and the hockey rinks were busy with youth teams wrapping up practices. In other words, there were vans, SUV's, and people everywhere. Ryan, overstimulated with the mass of vehicles and people, determined he would benefit from some alone time, so he parked by the walking path, went to his favorite bridge, and observed the action surrounding the factory from a safe distance. But this time, he reflected on the property from the perspective of an owner. He began to envision some expansion ideas and wondered if they could add more community-engagement opportunities if they cleared out a large grove of pine trees. He thought they could create at least another 800 square yards of public space without losing the scenic tree line that surrounded the acreage. He also thought they should check with the county about another entrance/exit route on the south end of the property. That would alleviate a ton of the congestion and allow the athletic teams and visitors a separate entrance away from the staff traffic. Ryan pulled out his phone and recorded a few of his visions for the property on his dictation app. His creativity and excitement grew as he allowed himself to dream, but it stopped when he saw Heather walk across the parking lot toward the rinks. Heather did not know Ryan was there yet, and he watched her greet the hockey coaches and gently remind them she needed the ice as soon as possible. She also made sure to say hello to the parents, anxiously waiting to get home with their future hockey stars. "She'll be a great Mrs. Claus," Ryan said aloud to himself.

Ryan stayed and watched Heather for quite a while. Like his new vision for North Pole, he realized he now viewed Heather as his future wife, not just his girlfriend. The thought brought a huge smile to his face as he meandered across the field to join her. When he was about 100 feet away, Heather finally saw him and gave him an exaggerated wave. Ryan waved back and wondered if he should give her a hello kiss. He debated the possibility without a conclusion until it was too late. Heather ran over and gave him a big hug and kiss before he even made it to the gate. His fears of Heather's reaction to any public display of affection were non-issues after she welcomed him in such a demonstrative manner. And there were plenty of people around who witnessed the hug and kiss, so word would spread fast. If she didn't care, neither did he.

Chapter 11

"This is going to sound corny," Ryan said as he slowly eased out of the embrace, "but I have missed you today."

Heather beamed, "Good," she exclaimed. "I'm glad. I missed you, too. Now, can I put you to work?"

"Of course; that's why I'm here early."

"Great. Will you please work with the coaches to get the goals and the practice gear in the storage shed and then run the Zamboni?" Heather knew Ryan loved to operate machinery and would be pleased to drive the ice-cleaning and resurfacing machine for 20 minutes.

"You bet!" Ryan responded affirmatively. "I wore my traction shoes tonight. Maybe I should have had them when we were at the gazebo?" They both laughed, and he made his way to the north end of the rink to grab that goal while Heather delegated more preparatory needs to her volunteers. The coaches already had the goal from the south end and were headed toward the shed.

Ryan loved the Model 100 Zambonis. They were much smaller than the ones used in the National Hockey League, but they were still a ton of fun to drive. The chore also gave him more opportunity to observe and admire Heather as she organized the event. There was open skating for the first 30 minutes, then the speed skating contest, and finally the figure skating. Sugar Grove was an ice skating community, and several of their skaters had made Olympic teams in the past, so there would be no awards for Ryan tonight, either. In fact, despite his history as a successful hockey player in both high school and college, he was only planning on skating for fun tonight. There might, however, be an award for Gabby – who supposedly was pretty good – in the 8 and under figure skating event. Ryan was embarrassed he had never seen her skate in person, even though he'd watched a few minutes of the videos Jennifer sent. *Should North Pole build an indoor skating facility to encourage even more young skaters?* he wondered, pulling out his phone and recording that idea, as well. He couldn't wait to share all these visions and dreams with Heather.

A few minutes into the open skate, the van with the rest of the family arrived. Ryan had changed into his skates and casually glided around the rink while remembering how much fun it was. He hadn't been on skates in years. As he slowed down and went to the entrance where Gabby and Henry were laced up and ready to join him, Gabby demanded to hold his hand and then so did Henry. Ryan now had his escorts for the evening and both kids were strong skaters already. Tucker didn't join them right away. He'd already had a two-hour hockey practice earlier in the day and his legs were tired. Gabe and Jennifer enjoyed their freedom from children and glided around the rink like newlyweds – and, like most Minnesotans, confident on their blades. Becky immediately jumped in to help Heather with the registration process. Ryan watched the two ladies working together while he and the kids skated around the rink and was so happy his future wife and his mother already had a wonderful relationship. *No in-law concerns in this relationship*, he thought with satisfaction.

After 15 minutes, Ryan convinced his two partners to leave the ice, but only after bribing them with hot chocolate. Heather and Becky smiled at the interlocked trio as they changed back out of their skates and then passed their table on the way to the concessions tent. Heather would be busy all night, so Ryan knew he wouldn't have the opportunity to talk with her privately. He was glad the ice cream cake was on the schedule at his mom's house afterward. He thought they might be able to take a stroll around South Pole to have some private time away from the family – well, everyone except Buford, who would definitely need a walk and some attention when they made it back home.

Chapter 11

While they sat drinking their cocoas, John Morrison approached their table. John was the chair of the board for North Pole and a family friend of the Millers. Ryan stood to shake his hand and John embraced him instead. John expressed his condolences. He had missed the memorial and the open house due to a family commitment overseas. Ryan was friends with one of John's sons, Robert, who now worked in London in the finance district. They had been in Sugar Grove Academy and Powell University together but had drifted apart the last decade. John wasn't one to mince words or engage in small talk, so Ryan knew he had ventured over for a reason. It became apparent quite quickly.

"Have you seen the ownership documents in your father's files yet?" John asked with an assumed affirmation.

"Yes, sir, I have," Ryan replied respectfully. "I was shocked and extremely honored to find out about my stake in the company." Ryan glanced down at

Gabby and Henry when he made the statement. John nodded his head in recognition of Ryan's nonverbal gesture.

"I am glad you are aware," John declared. "It was a spirited debate with your father when the decision was made. No one doubts your competence, Ryan," John continued. "It's your commitment to North Pole and Sugar Grove that has been, appropriately, questioned."

"Totally fair concern," Ryan agreed. "However, this week has revealed to me many reasons why this is no longer a warranted concern. It might take me a few months, but I am committed to a change in environment and habitation." Again, Ryan used words he hoped Gabby, a serious eavesdropper, wouldn't understand; Ryan had already been the benefactor of Henry's equal skill in this arena.

"Great to hear," John said. "I'll let you enjoy time with your family, but I'd like to invite you to Sugar

Grove Country Club for a brunch with me and a few other board members on Saturday at 10:00 a.m. Will that time work for you?"

Ryan had originally planned on leaving Sugar Grove on Friday, but now he didn't plan on leaving until Sunday at the earliest. "That would be fantastic. I look forward to that opportunity," Ryan confirmed. "I have many ideas and questions already, and I haven't even looked at my dad's computer yet. I'm sure I'll have more after a few hours in his office tomorrow."

John pulled out his wallet and gave Ryan his business card. "Call me anytime this week if you want to chew the fat a little before we meet with the others," John offered.

"I am sure I will take you up on that offer, sir," Ryan said, standing and shaking John's hand again.

"Call me John, Ryan. We are equals now and on the same team." Both men smiled at the comment. John then turned to head back to his wife and grandkids.

"Tell Robert I said hello," Ryan shouted while covering Gabby's ears, so it didn't startle her when he raised his voice and directed his communication right over her head.

"Sure will," John yelled back. "He is actually coming to town tomorrow. He is interviewing for the CEO role next week. He's tired of London."

That information startled Ryan, and he hoped John hadn't noticed. Robert was just as qualified to lead North Pole as Ryan was, so, for the first time in the last two days, Ryan's dream world had a pragmatic problem in it. He assumed Heather didn't know Robert was coming into town or she would have told him, but how could this not be news at the leadership level? He would ask her later tonight. This news would now require some quicker decisions than he had originally intended. If anything, his response to Robert's coming interview solidified what his heart had been leaning toward. He was 100% ready to move back to Sugar Grove.

Chapter 11

****

The skating contest went well, drawing a huge crowd. Henry watched the entire event from Ryan's shoulders and both his 50 pounds and his incessant encouragement for Gabby had given Ryan a massive headache. Gabby did very well and finished in 3rd place, quite impressive considering the two girls who finished ahead of her were both eight years old, two years older than his niece. Gabby wasn't fazed about not being first. She was super proud of herself and pinned her white ribbon on her red coat.

Everyone helped clean up, but after the crowd dispersed, Gabe, Ryan, Tucker, and Henry went back on the ice to pass the hockey puck around. Gabe had brought four sticks and Ryan was extremely impressed with Tucker's stick handling. He asked Tucker what time his team played this weekend, praying he would have time to see him play at least once. And of course, just his luck, Tucker's first game was Saturday at 10:00.

His second game was at 4:00, and the third game was Sunday at noon. Ryan committed to him that he would get to at least one of them for sure. Tucker was excited to hear this promise, as was Henry, who had invited himself to attend with Ryan if his mother allowed it.

About ten minutes into their hockey time, a couple of men joined the ladies at their table. It was Pastor Steve, who waved at Ryan when their eyes met, and a man Ryan did not recognize. Ryan hadn't seen Steve the whole night, so he assumed he had only come now with the other gentleman, which certainly peaked Ryan's curiosity. After a few more minutes, the hockey men decided to call it a night. Tucker had practice again at 9:00 the next morning and wanted to go to Grandma's to have some ice cream cake. The rest of them agreed and skated over to the exit.

They sat down together on the benches and took their skates off while they teased each other about their passing abilities or lack thereof. Gabe finished first, gathered the equipment together, and loaded it into his van. When he came back to join them, he had a very strange look on his face, and his countenance had changed. He looked worried and anxious. Ryan noticed and so did Tucker, but before either one of them could comment, Henry informed them of the shocking news with a scream of delight. "DAD!"

Chapter 12

Ryan's immediate response was disbelief, but when he caught a glimpse of Heather's face, he knew it must be true. She looked so uncomfortable and pained, her beautiful face contorted, almost as if she had suffered a stroke. His mom fared not much better. She had her arms folded and her face was expressionless, in a state of catatonic shock. Gabby, the only one not paralyzed in confusion, was dramatically communicating a recap of her skating performance to Josh and Pastor Steve. Gabe and Tucker had wandered over to the table to be by Jennifer, who was doing her best to be cordial, but she looked as if she wanted to jump across the table and strangle Josh.

Henry didn't even put his gym shoes on before he sprinted in his little sock feet to the table and jumped into his father's arms. Josh gave him a huge hug and showered him with kisses, which made Heather and

Jennifer even more upset. Ryan was stuck in his position. He hadn't moved a muscle this whole time. He hadn't even put his shoes on yet. He wanted to march up to the table and punch Josh in the face, but he was so perplexed by the intrusion he was numb. He stared at the table, desperately wanting to make eye contact with Heather, but she wouldn't look his way. Ryan finally started to put his shoes on and thought he might throw up. His mind was racing in all the wrong directions. Only Pastor Steve seemed comfortable, and for a moment, Ryan was seriously annoyed by his always peaceful spirit. After a few more minutes staring at the reunion, Ryan gained his composure and headed over to join the group, carrying Henry's shoes with him.

Josh was a handsome man and not nearly as small as Ryan had imagined, which was too bad. He had piercing blue eyes and curly black hair that peeked out of his knit hat, and a full thick beard. He looked naturally fit with broad shoulders. Josh had moved

Henry to the chair next to him and respectfully stood up to shake Ryan's hand, which also disappointed Ryan. He wanted a reason to dislike Josh more than he already did. "So nice to meet you, Ryan," Josh offered. "I've heard so much about you; it feels like I know you already."

Josh's grip was painfully strong, and Ryan managed not to grimace or twitch in response. Ryan was quiet for a couple of seconds and held on to Josh's handshake too long, sizing up his competition before he finally meekly replied, "The same with me." He couldn't tell Josh it was nice to meet him because it wasn't. It was, in fact, terrible to meet him, see him, or frankly to even know he was alive, let alone in the area. Finally, the two men released their hands and quit staring at each other. They were about the same height, though Ryan was probably a half an inch taller. Josh sat down again, and everyone looked at each other in awkward silence. It was Becky who finally broke the tension with a polite, but poignant question. "So, Josh, what brings you back to Sugar Grove?" Ryan stayed standing and was perched behind Gabe and Gabby, where he could watch both Josh and Heather.

"Well, Mrs. Miller," Josh answered while he smiled and looked at Heather and Henry, "my family." This disclosure only added tension to the chilly air and reception, and Ryan was pretty sure he let out a guttural sound of anguish.

Jennifer couldn't contain herself any longer and laughed sarcastically at Josh's statement while she rolled her eyes and looked away. "Let's get the kids home, where families are together." she announced to Gabe, and everyone knew it was a command rather than a suggestion.

Gabe seconded the order and told Tucker and Gabby to hug their grandma goodnight and follow him to the van. Jennifer gave Ryan a big hug and then went directly to Heather and did the same. Then she said loud enough for Josh and Steve to hear that she hoped her night was not ruined by the surprise. Josh was fortunate the kids were around, or Jennifer most certainly would have given him a long lecture about responsibility and commitment in marriage and family. Jennifer stared at Josh intently after she released Heather from her embrace and pointedly said goodbye to everyone except Josh while she never took her eyes off him. *Wow,* Ryan thought. *Remind me to never get on my sister's bad side! And, man, am I proud of her for sticking up for her best friend and her brother.* She also gave Pastor Steve a sarcastic, "Glad you could join us tonight" goodbye.

Heather had still not said anything or looked at Ryan since he and Henry had joined the group. Ryan stood there, holding Henry's shoes awkwardly at his side, too scared to sit down and feeling terribly out of place. There was a minute of strained painful silence. He wanted to interrogate Josh as much as everyone else did, but instead he eventually followed Jennifer's lead and decided it was best to leave. He went around the table toward Heather and told his mother he'd give her a ride home. Becky came with Jennifer and Gabe, but they had already left and had not remembered to take her. Ryan set the shoes down next to Heather and then leaned over to hug her goodbye.

Ryan didn't know what to say to Heather and she finally stole a look at him before his head went to the side of hers. She looked terrified, but there was nothing Ryan could do to save her from this moment. She had to face it, and they both knew it. Ryan whispered, "I love you" in her ear and gave her a kiss on the cheek. He hoped Josh saw the kiss but didn't really care if he didn't. The kiss was for Heather. It wasn't mean to intimidate or annoy Josh. Ryan gave a simple hand wave goodbye to Henry, Steve, and Josh, and held his mother's arm as they strolled toward his Corvette. Neither of them said anything until they were in the car.

Chapter 12

Ryan punched the steering wheel and leaned his head forward to rest on the top of the wheel as he softly screamed, "Everything was going so good. Why did he have to show up?"

"I know, Honey," Becky said quietly. "I'm so sorry. That was quite a shock. I still can't believe it. I trust Heather to navigate this nightmare and remain faithful to her heart."

"I think I would agree with you if she didn't have Henry," Ryan said dejectedly as he started the car and backed out of the parking space.

****

Heather watched Ryan and Becky leave and then asked Henry to sit by her. Pastor Steve excused himself from the table and offered to take Henry with him, but Heather rejected his offer. "Anything Josh wants to tell me in the next two minutes will be heard by Henry, as well," she said sternly while she glared at Josh. "We deserve some answers, but we also deserved a warning of your visit, and you have once again ignored my boundaries." Josh locked eyes with Heather, and, feeling the intensity of her anger, appropriately did not smile or offer any excuses.

Pastor Steve started to take some ownership of the surprise visit. "I am sorry Heather, this was. . . ." But Heather cut him off.

"Pastor," Heather said strongly, "I appreciate whatever role you've played in helping Josh with his life, but this surprise tonight was not appropriate or appreciated. I am glad Henry was able to see you again, Josh, but I am not about to change my entire schedule tonight, or this week, to listen to whatever excuses you have for deserting us."

Both men were a bit surprised by the firmness of Heather's response, but they shouldn't have been. The only reason Pastor Steve had agreed to the unannounced visit was because he believed it was the only guaranteed way Josh had to see Heather and Henry.

He couldn't explain all of that to Heather before Josh did, but he felt terrible for causing a disruption and obviously angering Heather.

"You're right, Heather, " Steve said apologetically. "I am sorry we didn't ask you if we could visit tonight. In hindsight, that was shortsighted and selfish. I am sorry."

"Apology accepted, Pastor," Heather said with a faint smile before turning and glaring at Josh.

"Josh, you have two minutes to make a brief statement about your life, and then I will need some time to consider further conversation. It took us over a year to recover from your departure, so you're not going to march right back into our life as if nothing happened."

Josh bowed his head, humbled by the reminder of the hurt he had caused his wife and child. He had obviously rehearsed his speech, but the passion of Heather's communication had shaken his confidence.

He looked at Pastor Steve for encouragement, receiving a gentle head nod in affirmation of his disclosure.

Heather, sensing whatever was about to be shared in terms of a confession was about to get serious, stopped Josh before he started with a raised hand. "Pastor, I think I will take you up on that offer to spend some time with Henry for a few minutes, so Josh and I can speak alone."

"Mom!" Henry complained, but Heather shot him a look that he obviously understood, and he immediately hopped off the chair and ventured toward Pastor Steve.

"Good idea," Steve said, relieved. He didn't want Henry to hear what was about to be shared, but it was Heather's decision. The two of them left, and as soon as they were out of ear shot, Josh unloaded his soul.

"Heather, I have been in rehab for the last year at the Minnesota Rehabilitation Center in Evergreen

Township. I was addicted to heroin and left you and Henry because I was in trouble and owed a lot of money to some very bad people. I left because they told me they were going to hurt you and Henry if I didn't give them the money I owed. I stole money from the city, paid them off, and left. I knew if I didn't leave, it would happen again and your lives were in danger." He looked at Heather, who had not expected drugs to be the main source of his struggles. He paused in case she had any questions or comments, and she did.

"Heroin?!?" she said, bewildered. "How long were you on it and when did you start?"

"I had been on heroin off and on since college. I hid it from everybody. I don't think anybody knew. I stole money from my parents to pay off my initial debts, but then I started drinking alcohol and soon became a drunk, as well."

Heather was dumbfounded, as shocked as she was angry. "Why didn't you tell me? Why didn't you ask for help?"

"I was embarrassed, humiliated, and didn't think I could ever beat it. I couldn't bear to admit to you how addicted I was," Josh offered humbly. "Like most hardcore addicts, I was in denial but also defeated at the same time."

"Did anyone at the station know? Did you ever tell them? Where did you go when you left us?" Heather asked, now curious about all the details despite her pain and frustration.

"No one at the firehouse knew, but the captain had started to get suspicious. When I left, I wandered around the Twin Cities in and out of drug houses and church missions. I was an absolute mess. It took me six months of homelessness and many near-death experiences to get me into rehab. I received some help from a pastor in Minneapolis, who hooked me up with the Rehabilitation Center, but I never paid a cent for my stay. I don't know who paid for me. It had to have cost well over $100,000."

Heather sat paralyzed in her processing. She didn't say a word for at least five minutes. She was really mad, and she was also really sad. Her natural compassion and her natural accountability and responsibility were at war with each other. Finally, she continued with more questions. "Why didn't you call me? Not even one time to give me an update, to let me know you were alive, to talk to Henry?" Heather's tears began to flow freely. "We thought you had left us because we did something wrong, not because you were a drug addict!" Her voice conveyed a mixture of contempt and compassion.

After a long pause, Josh finally shook his head and said softly, "I don't know. I felt like such a loser. You were this amazing woman, Henry was this beautiful boy, and I was drunk and stoned and living in the streets. But you guys were the motivation I needed to eventually choose rehab. I kept your picture with me in my wallet, and it stopped me many times from killing myself. In rehab, I posted it in my room for encouragement," as he pulled the worn picture out of his wallet to show her as evidence.

Heather, silent and bewildered, sat there in anticipatory apprehension, so Josh continued. "In rehab, you aren't allowed to talk to your friends and family, so none of my family, let alone anybody in Sugar Grove, knew I was there. Because I had drug and alcohol addiction, it took a whole year for me to get clean and to retrain my brain and my body to sobriety. And I stayed a little longer to train to be a sponsor myself," Josh explained. "Whoever paid for my stay told Evergreen to educate me on helping others through what I had experienced."

"Then how did Pastor Steve find out?" Heather asked indignantly.

"He just found out a few months ago and didn't know I was coming until two days ago, after I was released. I didn't know who to call, but I thought he was a safe man to start with even before I reunited with my family," Josh admitted sheepishly. "My parents aren't ready to see me yet and were polite on the phone but asked me not to come over. That really hurt. I desperately needed to see you and Henry, and I'm not sure I could have handled it if you guys rejected me also. That's why I talked Pastor into coming with me on this visit."

The two of them sat in silence for another minute. Heather tried to analyze the confession, but it was going to take her a while. She admitted to herself it was nice to have some answers finally, but the wound was opened again, and she'd had enough post-traumatic response for one evening. Her head hurt and her neck and shoulders ached. Josh sat quietly in a state of hope and fear. Finally, Heather tried to summarize what she was currently feeling.

"Thank you for telling me the truth, Josh, and I know it's the truth because it's too awful and too shameful to tell me if it was a lie. It *is* nice to have some answers, but it also brings many more questions to my mind, and I will need to process and ponder before we talk again. I also need to figure out how to tell Henry about your addictions without damaging him further – which frankly, I'm not sure is possible." She stopped as she contemplated that reality before continuing.

"May I have your phone number, so I can call you when I am ready to have another conversation?" she asked directly.

"I don't have a cell phone, Heather," Josh said quickly. "In fact, I only have a few changes of clothing, some books, and my toiletries. That's it. I don't have a home. I don't have a car. I don't have a family. I'm staying with Pastor Steve, and he is helping me try to find a new start somewhere, so I'm going to clean the church for a few weeks to make enough money to survive."

Heather recognized a man who had hit rock bottom and now had to dig out of an enormous hole. "I have some of your belongings in storage, Josh. I'll drop them off at the church tomorrow."

"Thanks," Josh said warmly. "I thought you had probably thrown everything out or burned it."

'Oh, I did burn a lot of your stuff," Heather said passionately, "but some of the items like your Vikings coat and your UM sweatshirt I just couldn't get rid of, even though I wanted to destroy them. I was going to give them to Henry when he was big enough to wear them. Speaking of Henry, I need to get him home and to bed. He is going to be elated and confused by your appearance. It will take me a while to decide how I will handle your existence in our lives again Josh. Give me time, please, to handle this incredible shock."

"Of course, of course," Josh said. "I am so, so grateful you were even gracious enough to listen to part of my journey. There's a lot worse stuff to share, but there's also some amazing ways that God intervened in my life and saved me. I've rededicated myself to Christ and believe my addictions are completely healed by Him. I am in AA meetings almost every day and stay connected with my sponsor and am totally dedicated to church and community again, as well."

Josh would have continued, but Heather put her hand up to tell him to stop. "That is all I can take tonight, Josh," she said, conceding to fatigue and stress. "I also can't touch you in any way so please don't expect a hug or even a handshake," Heather said sternly as she rose from the table and buttoned her coat. She was really cold now and needed to have a warm shower, curl up in three blankets, and call Jennifer.

"Understood," Josh said willingly. "Thank you for letting me share a bit and for allowing Henry to hug me and sit by me for a minute. It honestly has given me what I have longed for and prayed about for months. A reason to continue forward. To find my new purpose. God really does answer prayer." He got up and headed for Pastor Steve. "Can I hug Henry goodbye tonight?" he asked softly.

"Yes," Heather accepted, "as long as he initiates the hug first."

"Thank you," Josh said, smiling joyfully. Heather admitted to herself that despite the crazy story he had just shared, Josh did look at peace. He appropriately walked ahead of Heather and toward the concession tent 30 yards away. Heather shook her head slowly side to side, completely confused with the hurricane of emotions whirling in her heart and head. Then out loud to herself she said, "Oh my gosh! I have to call Ryan." She pulled out her phone and almost pushed his number, but she had no idea what she was going to say. "I better wait until after Henry is in bed and talk to Jennifer first," she said again to herself. She recognized the need to process more thoroughly this crazy development, and she wanted to hear Henry's response to seeing his dad. She finally shuffled through the snow toward Steve, Josh, and Henry, who were eating cookies and drinking hot chocolate.

****

Ryan and Becky had stayed silent the entire drive home. When they parked and headed up the driveway, Becky did her best to offer some maternal care. "Would you like something to eat, Honey?"

"Thanks, Mom, but I don't think I have an appetite. I feel nauseous. I need a stiff drink and then I'll take Buford on a long walk," Ryan mumbled dejectedly.

"OK," Becky said with as much love and compassion as she could. The truth was she didn't feel very good either and wanted to lay down and watch a

Hallmark movie, so she would be guaranteed a romance with a happy ending.

Buford waited at the door for them, and Becky offered to feed him so Ryan could have a moment to finish his drink and to switch shoes and coats. Becky came back in the kitchen and put her hand on Ryan's shoulder before she put some dishes from the sink into the dishwasher. Ryan was thankful for her presence and for her discernment not to muster up some trite notion of positivity. They both knew Josh's showing up had thrown an enormous monkey wrench into the week, the romance, and maybe even the future. There were a million ways this could end up, but Ryan wasn't thrilled about any of them at the moment.

After a few more minutes, Ryan said the magic words Buford anxiously waited to hear. "Go get your leash, boy," but then Ryan and Becky both had a healthy laugh and a much needed release of positive energy because Buford was already holding his leash in his mouth, patiently waiting for the walk to commence.

Ryan looked at his phone. It had been almost 40 minutes since he left the love of his life with the man who had received her love in marriage. He tried not to envision the two of them in a passionate embrace or the three of them sitting around the kitchen table sharing memories as a family, but his mind was racing out of control. He turned to his therapist for comfort.

"Buford," Ryan barked at his dog as they headed off the driveway and into the dark border that surrounded the property, "we have some things we need to talk about." Buford twirled his head back and forth to keep eye contact with his master while somehow keeping his balance to navigate the trails without tripping. Ryan wondered if he would be able to do the same with the path now laid out before him. "Confounding Event Outcome," Ryan told Buford as they turned to head around the back of the barn and toward the lake. "What is it about ice skating that is disastrous for Heather and me?" Ryan asked Buford, as if Buford would know.

Chapter 13

Heather and Josh ventured over to the concession tables where Steve and Henry sat anxiously waiting. Josh sat down beside Henry, who did indeed want to hug his dad, and he did so with the fervor of a boy who had not seen his father for over a year. Henry moved his chair as close to Josh as he possibly could and would barely take his eyes off him. Heather wasn't sure how they could eat their cookies and drink their hot chocolate in this entanglement, but she had to admit her heart was warmed by the scene. All the anger she had toward Josh didn't override the joy in her heart for Henry's opportunity to reconnect with his father. She knew at that moment if Josh kept himself clean and sober, she would need to allow this relationship to continue. It would be a hard choice to make, but it was the right thing to do for her son.

Pastor Steve invited Heather to sit with them, but she declined and separated herself enough from the three of them so she could observe and protect but not engage. Josh did a great job asking Henry questions about school and his Nintendo games and really listened to his answers. Heather was impressed. She realized, for the first time, she had never known this side of Josh and that she must now view her entire relationship with him through the lens of drugs. After about 10 minutes, Heather broke up the reunion, which disappointed all the men at the table. She was tired, cold, and emotionally exhausted, and she knew Henry had to be also. The skating contest responsibility was challenging enough without your ex-husband showing up for the first time in 16 months!

"Henry, we need to go home and get to bed," Heather said firmly, but with an understanding tone.

Chapter 13

"Aw, Mom," Henry whined, "I want to talk to Dad some more," and both Josh and Henry gazed at Heather with pleading eyes.

"Not tonight," Heather said quickly with more edge in her voice than she had intended. "If your dad is in town for a while, I promise both of you the opportunity to see each other some more." This revelation appeased Henry and Josh, and they each smiled broadly.

"Thanks, Mom," Henry said as he stood up and gathered his things together. He had managed to finally put his shoes on, but his feet had to be freezing.

"Thanks so much," Josh said as he approached Heather quickly, but Heather stepped back for space. Josh read the nonverbal response, remembered Heather's boundary, stopped abruptly, and finished expressing his gratitude from five feet away. "You have no idea how much this means to me. Your amazing character and faith shine even in the darkest hours,"

Josh said poetically. As he finished these remarks, Henry grabbed his hand to walk to the parking lot.

"Thank you. I think I do understand," Heather said warmly as she watched father and son reconnect.

Josh and Henry walked toward the parking lot, and Henry led the way to the Pathfinder. Pastor Steve came over to walk with Heather, but she shook her head, so he veered to the right and followed Josh and Henry without comment. Heather would have burst into tears if Steve would have said even a single word of blessing or gratitude. She'd held it together the entire night and was ready to have a meltdown. She would call Jennifer as soon as Henry was asleep, have a good cry, and ask for some insight on what to say to Ryan. She admitted to herself that she was glad to see Josh and observe some changes in his life, but her anger about the entire relationship was close to the surface and would take time to process into another round of healing. He had lied to her and hidden his drug addiction throughout their whole marriage. *How much of our money did he spend on that junk?* she wondered. She would forgive him, but she didn't want to get back together with him now or ever. That trust was completely eradicated and her romantic love for Josh could not be repaired. But Josh would need to be a part of their lives somehow – for Henry's sake. That was a tough reality to ask Ryan to accept, but she hoped and prayed he would be willing to live with that tension.

Henry hugged his dad goodbye, but Heather stayed back a bit and told Josh she would call Pastor Steve sometime tomorrow and drop off some of his things at the church. She also said she would prepare her requirements for interaction and communication. Both men thanked her again and turned to walk away as Henry ran over to his mother. "I love you, Dad," Henry shouted out to his father. The sight of Josh walking away must have triggered the need to declare his heart and rekindled his fear of abandonment.

"I love you too, Henry," Josh yelled back. "I can't wait to see you again. Goodnight."

"Goodnight," Henry replied, copying his dad's inflection perfectly.

"OK, Henry," Heather said with fatigue dripping from each breath as she helped Henry buckle into his seat. "Let's get home and get you a shower and to bed."

"OK, Mom," Henry replied excitedly and then grabbed her around the neck and pulled her in for an embrace that threatened to strangle her. "I love you the most, Mom," he whispered and didn't let go until Heather's neck and back started to hurt.

"I love you so much, Henry," Heather whispered, and unable to help it, the tears began to flow. Henry had melted her heart again. "I am so glad you were able to see your dad. We will figure out how to start this relationship again," she assured him as she removed his death grip from her weary shoulders.

Chapter 13

"You mean you are going to date dad again?" Henry asked as Heather shut his door and opened the driver's door for herself.

"No, Honey. I don't think I could ever date him or marry him again, but I meant your relationship with your daddy. If your dad continues to make good choices, then we will continue to make sure you get to spend time with him." Heather was formulating her position for explaining life to her inquisitive and perceptive five year old.

"OK," Henry responded. "I am so glad Dad came home."

"Well, Honey, I am, too, but just so you know, he is not going to live with us at home. He is staying at Pastor Steve's church," Heather explained. "Dad has been gone a long time, so I am not going to let him live with us. But as of now, he is home in Sugar Grove."

"OK," Henry said. "I'm still glad we got to see him and that I can see him again soon."

"Me, too," Heather conceded.

****

Ryan stayed out with Buford for about a half hour and was extremely disappointed he hadn't heard from Heather yet. The silence did not help his mood or his mental state, and he accidentally shut the deck sliding door pretty violently when he entered the back of the kitchen and stepped into the family room.

"Are you OK, Ryan?" Becky asked as she hurried into the kitchen from her back bedroom. She looked like she might have been already in bed.

"Sorry, Mom. I didn't mean to shut the door that loudly. I was lost in my thoughts, which aren't really pleasant right now," he said with some attitude. "I think I need a hot shower and a good night's sleep."

"I understand, son. I feel the same way right now, and it has nothing to do with you and Heather, though that certainly doesn't help," Becky said sadly. "I really missed your father today especially when Josh showed up at the rink. The absence of your father to talk about the drama of the day was very difficult. I've shed more than a few tears since you've been out with Buford."

"Oh, man," Ryan said and quickly went over to give his mother a hug. "I've been so wrapped up in my own issues I have completely neglected your heart and the grieving for Dad. I am so sorry. Please forgive me."

"Of course," Becky said as she wiped her tears with the sleeve of her robe. "Despite this crazy day, it has been so great to have you home this week."

"It has been fun," Ryan said genuinely, and then his phone rang. It was Heather. He showed his mom Heather's name on the screen, and she mouthed, "Good luck," and blew him a kiss as she turned to head back to her bedroom. Ryan waited another ring, took a deep breath, and tried to think of a clever hello to mask his trepidation.

"Well, that was an interesting night," he said as calmly as he could.

"You're not kidding," Heather replied soberly. "I am sure you realized I had no idea Josh was in town or that he was coming to the rink," she said with genuine innocence.

"Absolutely," Ryan said. "You should have seen your face. You looked like you had seen a ghost."

"That's what it felt like, Ryan. I honestly never thought I would see him again. I had already grieved the marriage like he had died," she disclosed painfully, and her voice cracked a bit. "Seeing him again was like a slap in the face or a punch in the gut."

"Well, after a few minutes, you looked like you were going to jump across the table and slap *him* in the face," Ryan said pointedly, "and Jennifer would have probably joined you if you had made a move in that direction," he offered, in an effort to bring some brevity to the intensity.

Chapter 13

Heather was silent for at least 10 seconds, so Ryan feared he had crossed the line with the retribution commentary.

"You have no idea how confusing this all is," Heather finally continued. "To have him just show up, seemingly ignorant of the impact of his disappearance, was unnerving."

"I can't imagine," Ryan admitted seriously. "Did he explain where he went or what he has been doing?"

"Yes, he did. And it was shocking. He was in drug and alcohol rehab for a year and had been addicted to heroin for our entire relationship," Heather said incredulously. "He was actually homeless for a while when he first left us. The people he owed money to actually threatened to hurt Henry and me. That's why he left."

This time it was Ryan who didn't speak for a while, though he was fuming inside. Finally, after some silence, he asked, "How are you dealing with all of this? That news couldn't have been easy to hear."

"No, it wasn't," Heather admitted quietly. After another long break, she said wearily, "I am absolutely exhausted, Ryan. I talked to your sister for 10 minutes and she helped me process some, but my mind is pretty fried right now. Could we just talk tomorrow sometime?"

"Sure," Ryan replied. "I have to ask two questions, though, so I can sleep tonight. I'm sorry these are pretty selfish at the moment, but Buford wouldn't give me a concrete answer."

"Of course," Heather said affectionately with a soft sigh.

"First, are you and Josh going to get back together? I need to hear it right away if my heart is going to be broken."

"No, we are not going to get back together, nor could I ever date him again, let alone be married to him," Heather said confidently, seriously brightening Ryan's mood and making the second question much easier to ask, even if he knew she was still in shock.

"Did Josh attend the Minnesota Rehabilitation Center?" he asked casually.

"He sure did," Heather exclaimed. "How did you know?"

"It's well known and used frequently for people in the Twin Cities," Ryan answered truthfully. "They are supposed to have a really good program and a strong faith base."

"Interesting," Heather said. "Josh appears to be genuinely clean, recommitted to Christ, and happier than I have ever seen him." She paused again, lost in wonder. After a moment, she gathered herself and said, with conviction Ryan appreciated, "I am sorry our night was ruined."

"No worries," Ryan said. "I sure was disappointed and, honestly, a bit freaked out, but then I put myself in Henry's shoes, and I was actually really happy for him . . . for both of them."

"Goodnight, Ryan Andrew Miller," Heather said softly, a bit ashamed she didn't have the same perspective right now, needing to get off the phone before she collapsed.

"Goodnight, Heather Ann Hayes," Ryan echoed.

****

Ryan woke up Thursday morning exhausted. Despite the knowledge Heather was not going to get back together with Josh, at least not right away, he had endured a fitful night of interrupted sleep, so upon waking, he laid in bed, staring at the ceiling and not moving a muscle for 15 minutes. He wondered how 24 hours could make such a drastic change in his mood, attitude, and future. "Buford, let's get up and get moving," he said more to himself than to Buford, but, regardless, Buford jumped out of his bed spryly, belying his age, and placed his head on the side of the bed for Ryan to pet him.

"Get your leash," Ryan commanded, and Buford sprinted out the door, down the hall, and toward the garage door. Ryan left the leash in the basket by the garage the night before, but it didn't really matter where he left it. Buford would smell and track his leash as if it were a varmint he was hunting. The longer trip for his leash gave Ryan time to dress, brush his teeth, and splash some water on his face as Buford returned and patiently waited by the bathroom door.

Ryan and Buford headed to the kitchen, and Ryan poured himself a cup of coffee, filled Buford's bowl and water dish, and checked his email on his phone. Buford, however, ignored his breakfast and paced back and forth across the kitchen floor, leash dragging behind him, scraping rhythmically with every turn. "OK, boy," Ryan said as he put his mug down, his phone in his pocket, and grabbed his coat and hat.

"Let's go," and they headed out the back door to the deck. "What are we going to do now, boy?" Ryan asked his dog as he shut the door behind them. "We have some serious decisions to make, and we really don't have much time." Buford was not a good listener that morning. He gave Ryan no eye contact as he pulled on his leash toward the fire pit.

****

Heather dropped Henry off at the sitter before eight, and, after a quick drive through a Dunkin Donuts for a large hazelnut iced coffee with cream, arrived at the North Pole. She had barely slept but was too wired to care and too confused to worry about it. She parked the Pathfinder in her marked space; though it was a really nice vehicle, she really missed her Honda. She sauntered across the lot and entered through the back door. Heather tried to say hello to all the co-workers she normally passed on her way to her office, but her heart and spirit weren't in the pleasantries this morning. She opened her office door and shut it behind her before letting out a deep sigh. She sat in her chair and opened her laptop, took a long drink of her coffee, and tried to switch mental gears to work mode.

She'd call Pastor Steve sometime later that morning, having solidified her plans after her sunrise breakfast and prayers. The more she'd thought of Josh's drug addiction, all the lies, and the endangerment of their lives, the angrier she became, and though she wanted Henry to have a relationship with his father, she would make Josh prove his responsibility and accountability slowly over time. Weekly supervised visits would be the extent of the relationship the first month, after church on Sundays from noon to six. If Josh didn't like it, that was too bad. This was all he was going to receive from them right now. He would not be allowed to call or text or just pop by until he had found a job and secured somewhere to live, and most of all, until Heather said he could.

****

Ryan showered and ate breakfast by himself. It felt as if he were back at his house in the city. His mother had left a note saying she had run into town to see some friends, and she'd be back around 10:00. Ryan checked his phone; it was 9:00. He had an hour of alone time and decided to investigate some more files on his father's computer. There was also something nagging him about what he had discovered in the financials on Tuesday, and he wanted to look at the expenditures again.

Buford followed Ryan, who took his coffee with him into his father's study. Turning on the computer, he brought up his dad's budget spreadsheets for both the personal and the North Pole ledger to see if he could reconcile the gifts to the Minnesota Rehabilitation Center he'd found in the donations file. *Could Dad have made large gifts to the Center to pay for Josh's recovery? And, if he did, why didn't he tell Heather about it?*

Sure enough, the two entries coincided with the times Josh had been at the Center. *Wow, this is fascinating. How did Dad know?* He stared at the screen and pondered this revelation.

Suddenly, Buford sprang off the floor and started barking before Becky had even reached the front steps, which startled Ryan back into the present. Buford waited for her by the door and, when she opened it, he greeted her as if she had been gone for weeks. Ryan met them both in the hallway and grabbed some bags from his mother, carrying them to the counter. He didn't waste any time with his questions.

"Mom, did you know anything about the two large gifts Dad made to the Minnesota Rehabilitation Center?" Ryan asked curiously.

"Yes," Becky replied.

"Did you know that Josh was at the Minnesota Rehabilitation Center for over a year and just checked out last week?"

Becky stopped moving and paused in a frozen stare. "No, I didn't."

"Heather told me last night Josh was a patient at the Center, and I had previously found two large gifts Dad made to them, one about 13 months ago and one about six months ago," Ryan reported.

"I wrote the second check, Honey," Becky admitted, "but I just assumed it was another one of the charities or agencies that had inspired your father to give. I didn't ask him what his reasons were or why he gave certain amounts. He had a list of commitments I made sure were completed, and I never bothered questioning or investigating."

"Do you think Dad knew that Josh was there?" Ryan asked with intrigue and wonder.

"I have no idea," Becky replied, "but, honestly, I wouldn't be shocked if he did. It would be surprising, though, if he withheld that information from Heather and me. You said Heather didn't know where Josh was, right?"

"She had no idea. She didn't know he even had a drug problem until last night," Ryan retorted indignantly.

"I'm going to see if I can find out," Ryan said as he pulled out his phone and looked up the Center. "I'm going to call them right now."

****

Heather called Pastor Steve right before lunch. They talked casually for about five minutes and then Heather peppered him with some specific questions.

"Did you know Josh was at the Minnesota Rehabilitation Center?" Heather asked pointedly.

"Yes, I did," Steve admitted, "but not right away. I only found out a couple of months ago."

"How did you find out?" Steve could tell Heather had the questions printed out before her or was reading them off her computer screen.

"Another pastor friend reached out to me," Steve answered. "He is a visiting preacher at the Center and struck up a conversation with Josh after one of the services. In fact, it was the service where Josh rededicated his life to the Lord. When Josh shared that he was from Sugar Grove, he asked Josh if he knew me, and Josh said he did." Steve paused for a minute to see if Heather had any response or additional question.

"Go on," Heather encouraged.

"The pastor called me and asked me if I would be a pastor Josh could connect with when he was discharged since he wanted to return to Sugar Grove," Steve continued. "I told him I was willing to serve Josh in that capacity and then just a few days ago, Josh called me and said he was coming to Sugar Grove."

"Why didn't you tell me about this?" Heather asked with some irritation in her voice.

"Three reasons." This time it was Steve who had prepared his words beforehand. "First, Josh asked me not to tell you. Second, we have pastor-parishioner confidentiality. Third, I have worked with many addicts, and until they show up and show themselves to be completely changed, you can't count on anything. There was no way I was opening that wound up to you and Henry until I saw Josh myself." Steve tried to share those truths with compassion, but he feared they came off too professionally.

"I know and appreciate the confidentiality," Heather said begrudgingly. "I certainly don't want you to share my story all over town, but I sure wish I would have received some kind of warning that he was coming back. I didn't have any time to prepare emotionally or mentally."

"I asked Josh to tell you Heather, but he wouldn't," Steve admitted. "He was pretty confident you would have denied him the chance if he had asked you directly."

"He's right," Heather acknowledged, "or I would have asked for a meeting with both of you privately first, and without Henry. Now, I feel that I have no choice but to allow the father-son relationship to continue. I'll break Henry's heart if I don't."

"I understand," Steve said genuinely. "I don't think he meant to manipulate you, but I can see in retrospect how that must have looked from your perspective. Are you willing to allow Josh an opportunity to earn a relationship with you and Henry? Have you thought through your boundaries for this process?"

"I have, and I would like to share them with both of you at the same time," Heather directed.

"Sounds good to me. Hold on. I'll go get Josh." Steve said quickly. "He's doing maintenance work for the church to pay off the initial loan the church gave him. We are paying for his meals and boarding, and we'll give him a check for the time and effort, as well."

"He told me all you and the church are doing for him," Heather affirmed. "I am glad you are working with him, Steve, but I am still a little disappointed in the way the surprise went down last night."

"I understand. For what it's worth, I thought you handled it magnificently," Steve said with genuine admiration. "You treated him with respect and grace but also kept control of the environment. It was very impressive."

"Thanks," Heather responded. "It may have looked strong, but I was a mess inside and still am."

"It will take time," Steve assured her. "No matter what you decide to do with Josh, your own heart and soul are going to need time to forgive and time to find a new rhythm as a family."

"I'm not sure we will ever be a family again, Pastor, but I am willing to make sure Josh is still a father if he stays clean, responsible, and appropriate," Heather reported with conviction.

"I totally understand. I've worked with many addicts, and it is definitely a journey. I'll find him and we can talk through the first steps. I'm going to put you on mute while I traipse through the church to find him." Steve didn't give Heather time to respond before she was muted. She wasn't sure what she would have said anyway, but she knew she had to talk to Ryan soon about all this.

Chapter 14

Ryan used his executive persuasion skills to move through several directors at the Minnesota Rehabilitation Center until he found the one who understood the significance of the Miller name. Becky was impressed with Ryan's initiative and urgency but was even more excited because Ryan identified himself as "son of Jim and new owner" of the North Pole Candy Company.

Ryan talked with the Vice President of Donor Relations, Alfred Olson for over 30 minutes and found out more than he had anticipated. Not only had his father given to the Center twice, but he also visited, and not during a fundraising dinner, either. He visited an addict in recovery named Josh, and the gifts Jim gave to the Center covered Josh's expenses for the year and allowed for a major renovation. Josh never paid a cent for his entire stay. Furthermore, Jim sent Josh a Bible and many devotional books shortly after he was admitted and checked on him via an email or call to his sponsor once a week until his accident.

Becky and Ryan were stunned with this news. They were proud and yet frustrated with Jim for the anonymity of the connection. Why would he hide it from Heather and Becky? Becky tried to remember if they had any conversations about Josh, but she could not remember any. "Your father might have purposely protected me from Josh's condition, knowing how angry and disappointed I would have been," she offered Ryan as a possible explanation.

As if Heather were listening to the conversation, Ryan's cell phone vibrated and he excitedly greeted her. "Hey Heath, Mom and I are here, and I am going to move you to FaceTime so we can both see you and share more updates we have for you."

"OK," Heather said, although she was not looking forward to more surprises.

Chapter 14

Ryan walked her through what he had discovered, and Heather was emotional about the revelation, though she didn't know if she should be happy, sad, angry, or joyful. "I don't know how much more new information I can take right now," she told Becky and Ryan while choking back tears and putting her head in her hands, "but I am glad to know the truth. Josh told me somebody had paid for his recovery, but I never would have guessed it was Jim."

"We had no idea about this," Becky assured Heather for both of them. "Ryan just found out through some detective work in Jim's office and a conversation with the rehabilitation center."

"I wonder why he didn't tell me?" Heather asked.

"I have no clue, but I will try to piece it together with more digging," Ryan assured her.

Becky interjected, attempting to refocus the conversation on the new relationship, not the old one.

"Are you two going to the Christmas cookie contest tonight?"

Ryan had completely forgotten about the contest, but it used to be one of his favorites.

"I have to be there," Heather responded, "and Henry can't wait to go. Last year he ate so many cookies he got sick, so this year we have a five-cookie limit."

"I'll bring Mom and keep her on a five-cookie limit, as well," Ryan replied dryly while grinning at his mother.

"I already told Henry you would go with us, Ryan, but I could let him know something came up if you already have committed to your mom."

"Nonsense," Becky piped in. "I am scheduled to be with Jennifer. Ryan is free to be with you two, and we'll all see each other there."

"OK," Ryan said. "I'd love to go with you guys. What time do you need me to be there?"

"5:30," Heather responded.

Chapter 14

"Alright. Sounds great," and Ryan managed his first smile of the day.

****

Josh had received the boundaries without complaint, debate, or consternation. He just wanted to start the visits right away this upcoming Sunday. Heather had planned to wait a week since Sunday was the day after Christmas, but because Josh respected her structure so willingly, she conceded and agreed they could go to Tucker's hockey game together. Heather hated to have the first visitation be in public. The small town gossip chain would get a fresh dose of Christmas conversation. Heather didn't agree, however, to Josh's second request, which was to sit together in church. Henry always left halfway through the service for children's church, and she wasn't comfortable sitting just with Josh, the two of them together in the pew. He understood. Heather also asked there not be any presents this first Christmas. She said that more for

Josh's sake than for Henry and her. She knew Josh didn't have any money. After Heather had ended the call, Steve and Josh ordered their lunch and discussed possible jobs and places for Josh to live in Sugar Grove. Steve encouraged Josh to meet with the Sugar Grove fire chief about possible reinstatement, but Josh wasn't sure he wanted a job with those crazy hours anymore. He was afraid of the impact that schedule might have on his sobriety.

****

Ryan arrived at Heather's at 5:00. He could have been there by 3:00 he was so excited to see her again. Heather wasn't quite ready, so Ryan and Henry had a conversation in the living room after she went back upstairs to her room. "Was it good to see your dad last night?" Ryan asked him genuinely.

"It was awesome. I hadn't seen him in a long time."

"I know. I am glad you were able to spend some time with him. When will you see him again?"

"Sunday. Mom is only letting Dad see me on Sundays after church. We will go to Tucker's hockey game together."

"OK." Ryan was impressed with Henry's understanding of the boundaries already.

"Mom isn't going to date dad anymore. She still wants to date you," Henry said with a big smile. "I want her to date you, too!"

"Well, that is really good news," Ryan said with great relief. Henry might just clear up every question for which Ryan needed answers before he even had to ask Heather. "I want to still date your mom also," Ryan admitted.

"Dad isn't going to live here either," Henry continued. "Mom can't trust him anymore."

"That sometimes happens with families after divorces," Ryan acknowledged and prayed Heather arrived soon before the conversation went beyond his comfort level.

Henry turned the tables on Ryan. "Gabby said you've never been married. How come?"

"That's right, I haven't. Well, to tell you the truth, Henry, I should have married your mother a long time ago and I didn't. And I've never been able to find anybody as awesome as she is."

"I think you should marry Mom now," Henry said with encouragement.

"I am thinking about it," Ryan said. "But I need you not to tell anybody about that, OK?"

"OK. I promise."

"Promise what?" Heather said with great curiosity as she skipped down the last few stairs and entered the room. Ryan looked a bit startled and nervous. She wore a sweater Ryan had given her almost a decade ago. She wanted to see if Ryan noticed.

Chapter 14

"I promised Uncle Ryan not to tell anybody . . .," Henry offered.

". . . About our secret," Ryan interjected as he interrupted and smiled at Henry.

Both men had cheesy grins on their faces, so Heather knew something significant had happened, but she let it alone for the time being.

"We are still early, guys," Heather commented, looking at her phone. "What do you want to do with our extra time?"

"Let's go eat a quick dinner at Flo's Diner," Ryan suggested. "I'm super hungry. I just started to get my appetite back about an hour ago," he admitted with a wistful and knowing look at Heather.

"Me, too," agreed Heather. "It may be busy, but if we can grab a table, I'm sure we can be in and out in 30 minutes."

"Awesome," Henry chimed in. "I love their kids' meals."

"Nice sweater," Ryan shared, grinning as he helped Heather with her coat. "I bet your former boyfriend bought that for you. Remember that selfish guy who didn't appreciate you enough?"

"I sure do. I've heard he's back in town and has made some major life changes."

"That's right," Ryan affirmed. "He always had good taste, however. That sweater looks great on you."

"You look beautiful, Mom," Henry agreed. "Ryan bought it for you, didn't he?"

Both Heather and Ryan looked at each other and shook their heads.

"Yes, he did, smarty pants," Heather affirmed. "Let's go eat at Flo's and then make some cookies." Heather grabbed the bag off the counter which housed her baking materials for the cookies.

As they walked down the walkway, Henry grabbed Ryan's hand and then grabbed Heather's hand.

Instead of holding them each for himself, he put their two hands together.

"Thanks," Ryan offered, "but I want to hold your hand also."

"Awesome," Henry declared and scampered to the other side of Ryan so that Ryan could still hold his mother's hand too.

****

Pastor Steve checked on Josh before he and his wife went to the cookie contest. Josh had painted most of the Fellowship Hall in the basement and it looked great. "When you finish this room, please shut it down for today," Steve encouraged him. "You have completed a lot of work. Take a shower, eat, and rest a bit. Renee brought you a sandwich and some chips."

"Thanks," Josh answered without taking his eyes off his roller. "It will be easier to paint than to sit by myself and think of Heather and Henry at the cookie contest without me."

"I understand, but part of your recovery and renewal is to allow those consequences to be a part of your new life without letting them define you or dictate your mood."

Josh was silent for a minute and Steve turned to leave. "You are right, Pastor. I will clean up after this room and start again in the bathrooms tomorrow. Thanks for the food and the work . . . and for everything."

"You're welcome. We're glad you are home and starting over. It will take time to build a new life, Josh, so try to be patient," Steve shared over his shoulder with a head nod of affirmation and a goodbye.

It took Josh another 20 minutes to finish the room, clean up, and return the equipment to the custodial closet. He showered, ate his dinner, and, instead of watching television in the youth room as he did most nights, went to the church library, took out a legal pad, and began to write a letter.

Chapter 14

****

The cookie contest was the last and most popular Christmas contest at the North Pole. As with every one of their contests, there were three categories for the awards: best tasting cookie, most original cookie, and best decorated cookie. Of all the events. This was the longest because everyone had to bake their cookies in the North Pole kitchens under the supervision of the North Pole staff bakers. The winner of the best tasting cookie category became the following year's North Pole new cookie for mass production. This award, therefore, was worth several thousand dollars, so once you won, you were automatically eliminated from participating again. The money, bragging rights, and constant new winners kept the contest fun and interesting – and meant Becky and Jennifer were not in the competition. They had both won years before, though Becky donated her check back to the kitchen for new equipment.

There were three different times for the contestants: 5:00, 6:15, and 7:30. Each group had up to 20 teams. This year there were a full 60 teams participating, so the competition would be steep. The cookies were tasted by the judges when they were warm and right out of the oven, but the display for the public and the community votes didn't happen until 9:00. This was the only contest for which everybody who attended had a vote, including the other contestants. The only rule was the contestants couldn't vote for their own cookie.

Ryan, Heather, and Henry had received a 6:15 spot and planned on a cookie Heather wanted to introduce to the North Pole bakers the past several years but had never been confident enough to suggest – a peanut butter and chocolate marshmallow cookie that tasted like a S'more. Heather had stumbled across the combination a couple of summers ago at a cookout when she ran out of graham crackers for the sandwich borders of the S'more and used peanut butter cookies instead. Ryan hadn't tasted them yet, but Henry said they were amazing.

To make her S'more cookies match the qualifications of the contest, Heather had to mix the chocolate and marshmallow together so that nothing additional outside of icing could secure the taste. She had experimented with a chocolate marshmallow icing, but it wasn't nearly as good, so she stayed with the batter mix, allowed the marshmallow to solidify with the chocolate, and chilled it for 45 minutes before she rolled and baked them. They would need the entire 75-minute timeframe to make sure they were as delicious as they should be, which would make their cookie execution tight.

The so-dubbed "Happy Henrys" looked beautiful out of the oven, and the judges seemed pleased and surprised with their look and taste. Usually, that was a good sign, but now came the hard part – they had to wait another two hours for the competition results and the 9:00 revealing to the public with the community votes. Heather felt fairly confident they would earn a spot in the finals in the most unique cookie category, but she was wrong. They earned two spots! They ended up in the most unique cookie *and* the best tasting cookie categories.

Chapter 15

Josh Thomas was the youngest of three ornery and rambunctious brothers. They were two years apart but looked so similar they could almost pass as triplets. Josh grew up mean and aggressive – and he was the nicest of the three boys. Sam was right above Josh, and he used to eat glass and catch squirrels with his bare hands. What he did with the squirrels afterward is too disturbing to mention. Gene was the oldest and toughest of the three. He treated his younger brothers like slaves and threatened to hurt them anytime they didn't do exactly as he said, and those were not idle threats. When the boys hit puberty, their fights were pay-per-view worthy with so many emergency room visits the nurses knew them each by name. There was a strong bond between the three, even if they beat the tar out of each other. Those wounds were nothing compared to what happened to anybody in the community who picked on one of them separately. If you bothered one Thomas boy, you received the wrath of all three in return. It happened only once, and the beating Cedric Hubbard earned for stealing Sam's lunch money in 8th grade put fear into the masculine community of Sugar Grove Junior High and High School for the remainder of the Thomas brothers' tenure.

The three men were serious addicts before they finished being boys. This shouldn't have surprised anybody because Jack Thomas, their father, was a life-long alcoholic, who stayed present with his family but in every way imaginable was a negative influence. Jack started his day with a beer, moved to mixed drinks by lunchtime, and the hard stuff by dinner. The boys hoped he would pass out by sundown, or the torment soon followed. Jack used his belt for discipline whether it was a serious offense or an accidental mistake, and sometimes just for fun. Jack had been beaten by his father, who had been beaten by his father, and they honestly thought it was the way to install respect and toughness in their sons. The boys were ultra-competitive and capable athletes, but they couldn't achieve any lasting success due to disagreements, arguments, and confrontations with teammates, coaches, and other teams.

Joan Thomas was a timid woman, who gave up on hope and peace 30 years ago. She tried to counter the anger and alcohol of her husband with sweetness and leniency, but that only made the chaotic environment more toxic, especially after Jack started to beat on her, as well. Joan wanted to leave Jack, but she didn't know any other life and hadn't held a job since she was 14. Joan had been in treatment for clinical depression and was so heavily medicated it was hard to remember what her true personality was like. In their late sixties, Jack and Joan seemed to be at least content now, though their bodies were failing them pretty quickly due to the hard life they'd lived and the toxicity of alcohol and drugs that ravaged their internal organs. They had no relationship with their adult sons, their extended family, or, for that matter, anybody in the community. Their marriage at this point was simply about routine and survival. It made Josh really sad.

Though he was highly decorated for his service, Josh's oldest brother Gene was a dishonorably discharged Navy SEAL after he nearly beat to death a couple of rowdy civilians in an Afghanistan bar. Gene had left the family as soon as he turned 18 and, subsequently, after he punched his dad in the face while defending his mother. The punch knocked his father out cold, and before he became conscious again, Gene went to his room, packed his bags, and left. He didn't say a word to his mom or his brothers on his way out the door. For several years the military gave Gene the structure and affirmation he needed, but soon his old demons resurfaced, and the Seal training and even the combat missions couldn't soothe the wounds of his soul and he self-destructed. The civilian incident was the final straw, but that was after several in-house discipline issues. Gene had married at 19, a runaway named Sissy, whom he met at a strip club during basic training. The marriage didn't stand a chance, and they were divorced before Josh left for his first mission. Content with nature and isolation, Gene now lived alone in the Florida Panhandle doing construction and, like many vets, mostly kept to himself. Josh hadn't seen or talked to Gene in about five years, but he wanted to visit him soon. He thought it was about time to reconnect, but he had other more important matters to work though first.

Sam was the middle brother and was addicted to weed and paint thinners by age 12, then slid into heavier drugs by high school. He died of an opioid overdose when he was just 21. Josh was 19 at the time and a freshman in college, and through his mandatory counseling in rehab now understood Sam's death was the tipping point of his soul consternation. Sam was Josh's best friend – really, his only friend – and he was devastated. Sam and Josh used to fight each other as a hobby, practicing mixed martial arts. Sam wanted to try out for the MMA after high school but couldn't get sober enough to give it a fighting chance. Josh never dealt with Sam's death, and his own heroin use started shortly after the funeral. No one but the immediate family knew Sam's death was an overdose. They told everybody, including Heather, that Sam had died of a rare condition that caused sudden cardiac arrest, though most people assumed there was more to the story.

Josh begun to journal in rehab about his wildly dysfunctional family and was now a prolific writer where processing his pain and heartache was concerned. When he finally acknowledged all the hurt from his youth, he cried every day for nearly two months. He thought he had gone soft and lost his manhood, but his therapist helped him understand this emotional release was actually called healing. Josh was now free with his tears whenever they were appropriate, but he still had a pretty sharp temper, and he was worried about losing his cool sometime again. Writing gave Josh understanding about who he was and what he had been through, and, in times when he was overwhelmed, like now, writing helped him make sense of his reality. It also kept his anger at bay.

Josh decided after seeing Heather and Henry again to write a series of letters to those he loved. These letters would not be explanations, excuses, or simple apologies. They would be laments (a word he now liked to use from the Bible), where he fully acknowledged the pain and heartache he had caused everybody. But the letters would also be redemptive. He would write about hope and his commitment to be the best son, brother, father, and friend he could be. They would not be meant to manipulate, coerce, shame, or rationalize – the kind of skillful communication all addicts master. His father had become sober a few years after Sam died but still remained imprisoned to his regret, guilt, and failures. Josh would choose a sobriety that inspired and impacted others in joy and peace and hoped to help his father heal by showing him an example of true freedom. The first letter started with, "Dear Dad."

****

The community tasted all the cookies while the judges tabulated the scores from the community with their own ledger to discover the victors. Hardly any of the 300-plus Sugar Grovians had left the Events Center. Ryan, Heather, Henry, Gabe, Jennifer, Gabby, and Tucker all waited, huddled around their tables, in nervous anticipation. Eventually it was Becky who sauntered across the stage and was handed a microphone by John Morrison. Becky nervously read the winners of the first two categories and the audience responded with the obligatory appreciation and affirmation, but everyone was there to witness the grandest prize of the North Pole Christmas Contest week. Finally, after some extra seconds to let the crowd stir even more, Becky read the name of the big winner.

"The winner of the 2021 North Pole Best Tasting Cookie Contest is . . . Heather Hayes and her 'Happy Henry' cookies!" Becky beamed, and a huge roar of applause erupted from the center, shaking the walls. Heather, Henry, and Ryan stood in frozen joy and then joined together for a celebratory embrace. Ryan instinctively and unashamedly gave both Heather and Henry a kiss on the cheek. Becky continued over the drone of the crowd. "Heather and Henry, please come to the stage to receive your trophy and then head over to the table on my left to meet with our comptroller, Luke Johnson, who will walk you through the paperwork and contract for the new 2022 North Pole cookie! Congratulations again, Heather and Henry!" Again, a loud round of applause from the audience made it difficult to hear, and Heather and Henry surfed their way through the crowd and the maze of tables toward the front of the room. Halfway there, however, Heather stopped and bent down to say something to Henry. He nodded his head in agreement and turned and ran back to the family table.

Henry stopped in between Gabe and Gabby and shouted across the table at Ryan so he could be heard over the clapping. "Mom wants you to come with us!"

Heather knew Ryan wouldn't turn down the invitation if it was from Henry. She was right. Ryan quickly complied, scampered around the table, scooped Henry up in his arms, and jogged to join Heather and made their way to the stage. Heather received the trophy from Becky and John and held it up over her head in an appropriate championship pose. Though excited, she was rarely this gratuitous in public expression, but this had been an enormously difficult week, and she released some stored-up energy in the moment. She was also beloved by the community as one of their own. Everyone knew her story – her parent's tragic death and her husband's disappearance – so it felt like community catharsis and retribution of fate.

Henry held on to Heather's hand and in his other hand was Ryan's. Becky asked Heather if she had anything to say, but she waved her head vigorously side to side in an emphatic "no." Henry, however, dropped his hand from his mother's and reached toward Becky. Becky gave him her hand, but Henry pulled her near and whispered something to her. He wanted to share something with the crowd and asked Becky if he could. She agreed, kneeling down to hold the microphone close to Henry's mouth. The crowd immediately quieted to hear the five year old's reflection on the win.

"These cookies are named after me," Henry proclaimed confidently, provoking applause and laughter. Henry paused and waited for them to listen again. "I'm a happy boy and these are the 'Happy Henry's.'" He beamed and the audience roared even more in laughter and the joy of watching the little ham on stage. Once more he waited for their attention. Maybe this was the start of Henry's career in public office. He had them eating out his hand. "I hope Mom's cookies make everyone as happy as me." Then he turned and gave his mother a huge hug, an emotional sentiment mixed into his message, and the crowd melted in the moment.

Becky stood back up and started to return to the center of the stage, but Henry shouted for her to wait and waved her back to him. Becky looked at John who, not about to silence a child who had the crowd captivated, nodded his head in approval. She returned to Henry and leaned the microphone down to him. "One more thing. Uncle Ryan has something to say to everyone," Henry proclaimed and looked at Ryan expectantly. Henry was making a habit of following the promptings of his heart regardless of the circumstance or situation. Becky smiled and stood up and moved over to Ryan with the microphone. There was no way Ryan could escape this moment. In these kinds of situations, his father and grandfather had been masterful and mesmerizing. They could spontaneously and reverently bless the North Pole community with words of grace and appreciation without written notes and without pretense or condescension. Ryan took a deep breath, accepted the microphone from his mother, and tried to follow in their footsteps.

"North Pole and Sugar Grovians, it has been an incredible joy to be back with you in this community this week. You have honored my father and my grandfather with this wonderful week of contests and celebration, but even more so with the amazing show of support and love at my father's funeral and open house." A respectful applause followed this first disclosure. Ryan continued, "My grandfather started this company with purpose and passion and loved you with his whole heart. He envisioned this community we now have, and what a legacy he left us. I miss him so much, and I bet you do also." The audience was quiet, did not respond in any fashion outside of some head nods, and was a little surprised by the testimony from Joe's wayward grandson. Ryan sensed the emotional tension and lightened the mood for a second. "Santa Joe is smiling down at us from heaven, though he is probably busy convincing the angels to try his newest candy." Everyone politely laughed, but Ryan wasn't finished bearing his heart. "And my father Jim would be ecstatic that this week has been about the joy of the Christmas season rather than about him. He'd enjoy that we continued the contest traditions and celebrated his life as if he were still living – because he is, with Jesus, and his and Joe's spirit is here with us helping us celebrate." This declaration shocked everyone, even Ryan, for he had never been public or vocal about his faith. In the crowd, Pastor Steve gripped Renee's hand tightly. Several of Ryan's former Sunday school teachers watched and listened with pride.

The surprises continued. Ryan was already knee-deep in confession and might as well finish. "I left Sugar Grove about seven years ago, and I am sorry for my distance, my arrogance, and my stubbornness about the beauty of this community." There was complete silence now as they listened to a private man bear his soul publicly. "I apologize for not carrying on the tradition of my grandfather and father and vow, from now on, to proudly identify myself with my heritage and my people. Please forgive me and allow me to re-enter the North Pole and Sugar Grove family." There was stunned silence in the center as Ryan looked at them and then simply said, "Thank you from the bottom of my heart."

Ryan handed the microphone back to his mother, who handed the microphone to Heather. Becky had tears streaming down her face and gave Ryan a warm and affectionate embrace. Heather was also crying as were about half of the people in the crowd who had watched Ryan grow up and remembered his following his grandfather and father around the campus. The silence was only interrupted with sniffles and the sounds of purses opening and hands digging for Kleenex. Heather handed the microphone to John so she and Henry could join the embrace. John wisely gave the tender moment some time and then addressed the audience, who were in an awkward space of what to do next.

"This has been an incredible evening of competition and community. And on behalf of North Pole, I celebrate the return of one of our native sons, the grandson of our founder, and the son of our recently deceased CEO. Let's give Ryan a North Pole homecoming with one more round of applause." The crowd, relieved to have something tangible to do, gave a nearly one-minute ovation. John continued, "Thank you for this great evening. Those of you who can, please stick around and help us clean and rearrange the room. Good night." The crowd once again erupted in heartfelt cheers as Ryan, Becky, Heather, and Henry made their way across the stage to Luke for the signing of the contract for the Happy Henry's.

Community Empathy Offering, Ryan thought to himself with deep relief in his soul as they walked across the stage he had played on when he was a boy.

Chapter 16

Josh and Heather met through tragedy, and their marriage was branded in post-traumatic stress for all five years. Josh was on the first engine called to the accident where Heather's parents had died. Their first conversation was at the funeral when the entire Sugar Grove Fire Department paid their respects. There weren't many vehicular fatalities in Sugar Grove, so the tragedy was a big ordeal, and the funeral drew a large crowd. Josh approached Heather at the grave site when she was alone, leaning against a tree, and staring into the sky. Josh gently offered his condolences and touched her forearm. Heather turned to face him and then collapsed into his arms and wept. Heather was weak and vulnerable, and Josh was lonely and angry. They were drawn to each other for needs neither understood.

The first months were simple and romantic, but the trauma made trust challenging, and Josh felt ill-equipped for a committed relationship. His drug use, though hidden, was mostly recreational during their dating and engagement and even into the early days of the marriage, and he created a false persona to survive the intimacy pressure. He appeased and comforted Heather but never shared his inner heart or soul. He routinely lied to her about everything, even mundane and unimportant things, and almost believed them himself. Josh wasn't really interested in getting married but decided he probably should after the boys at the firehouse constantly needled him about it. He bought a cheap ring and asked Heather unromantically after they had finished a 5K together, exhausted and sweaty, standing around in the parking lot. Heather accepted Josh's sudden marriage proposal because she didn't know what else to do. She was afraid to be alone, and Josh had conveniently filled that void. She did grow to love the man he pretended to be; she just didn't know the fullness of his pathology.

Chapter 16

The handsome, but unhealthy couple were married a year and a half after the accident, and even on their honeymoon Heather felt something was off, but she never guessed Josh used drugs. The first year was fine – nothing terribly wrong, but nothing wonderfully right, either. They developed a workable routine based on Josh's hectic schedule and the fact that firemen's spouses have several days a week when they are alone. The days they were together were filled with recreational activities – camping, hiking, tennis, ice fishing, skating, and bowling. Staying active and involved kept Josh engaged and kept Heather from focusing on her broken heart. Rarely would the couple talk through their daily lives or the dreams and desires of their career. They were good roommates and complementary companions, but there was no true intimacy or depth of relationship.

Josh would often take five or ten minutes to himself during their outings, but Heather didn't think anything strange about it. Josh was a loner and, though socially fun, was actually quite introverted and shy. Heather never dreamed those moments allowed Josh to be alone with his drugs. When she looked back in retrospect at their entire history together, it was as if scales fell from her eyes, and every significant issue or event was now seen through the lens of addiction. Heather had enabled an addict in her home and in her heart but didn't know it and couldn't do anything about it. The fire house was just as shocked as Heather when Josh disappeared, but if anyone had been able to see into Josh's heart and soul, escaping from Sugar Grove would have been a logical conclusion.

Around the time real marital issues began to surface, Heather became pregnant with Henry. The excitement and nerves around the coming baby stopped the couple from working through their problems. Heather's pregnancy was not easy, and she didn't feel well through the first two trimesters. Josh was at a loss how to care for his homebound and inactive wife and often paced around the house like a caged lion. Josh was also really scared to have a child because he had no positive parental role models or any experience in a happy home. Heather's parents had doted on her and raised her with such autonomy and freedom she never recognized Josh was struggling with the pregnancy and impending fatherhood. The closer the due date, the more Josh disengaged and shut down. He even missed a few of their parenting classes. Josh told Heather it was because of emergencies at work, and why would Heather doubt that lie? Every fire or 911 call Josh responded to was an emergency. The truth, however, was Josh was cracking under the pressure of work, marriage, and the movement into parenting, and his recreational drug use became regular and habitual and eventually went out of control.

Though the pregnancy was difficult, Henry's delivery was thankfully easy, and Josh and Heather celebrated their newborn baby with just Jennifer, Gabe, and the fire chief. The absence of either set of parents during this enormous rite of passage profoundly impacted Heather, and after they returned home, she quickly slid into post-partum depression. Though it was an awful month and a half, this ended up a blessing when the depression, and the tears of care from Jennifer, inspired Heather to seek counseling, where she finally began to unload her soul and process through the devastating and sudden death of her parents. As Heather healed and recovered, she encouraged Josh to seek counseling to deal with the death of Sam and his terrible childhood, and though Josh admitted he needed it, he never went – not even once – and Heather never demanded it or took him there herself. They were both afraid of what might be unearthed or revealed in therapy.

Josh tried to be a good father, but he didn't have a clue how to be affectionate to a baby. Josh would hold Henry for five or ten minutes, but the baby might as well have been a sack of groceries. There was no softness or tenderness in his hold or his heart. Josh always had a good reason for why he quit holding Henry so quickly, and Heather didn't press him about it, but there was never a father-son nap or casual time of admiration and awe at God's gift of life. The only time Josh could give Henry prolonged attention was if they were on a power walk. Josh pushed the stroller so fast, however, Heather found it not relaxing and eventually gave up and let Josh run with Henry himself. She used that time to rest and catch up on her emails.

When Henry began to walk and talk, Josh would seem excited but distant, almost like he was afraid something would go wrong, or he would hurt Henry if he played with him too hard or for too long. It was obvious he loved Henry, and he did manage to give him a hug and kiss every night he was home, but Heather could see it was a painful process for him. Heather never worried about Josh hitting Henry, but Josh would often lose his temper over things Henry couldn't control and often yelled for no apparent reason. Heather compensated for the father deficiencies where she could, but she knew Henry needed more masculine time and that's when she started to visit Jim and Becky. And oddly enough, Josh seemed to enjoy the times when he was with Jim and Becky also, though those were few and far between. Heather normally spent time at South Pole when Josh was on overnight duty. Unbeknownst to Heather and Becky, Jim noticed signs in Josh that weren't healthy or appropriate and began to check in on him at the fire house. Jim was good friends with the fire chief; they were deacons together at the church. This gave Jim access to some inside information about the valuable, but intensely impulsive, driver engineer of the Sugar Grove Fire Department.

Heather knew something was seriously wrong when Josh started to lose interest in sex. At first, she thought it was just his fear of having more children, but eventually it was obviously much more than that. Sex had always been a calming influence in their marital life and then suddenly, after Henry turned three, Josh didn't seem to need it anymore. This culminated with even more erratic behavior and communication. Heather kept faith in Josh and made excuses to Jennifer and co-workers who began to question his lack of presence at North Pole parties, events, and celebrations. It was about this time, shortly before Josh left, that Heather sought counsel from Pastor Steve. Josh had quit attending church, and after one service Steve privately asked her about it. Heather admitted there were some significant issues and asked to come and talk to him. They met a couple of times a month through the disappearance, the divorce, the depression, and the recovery. Heather's understanding of herself, loss, grieving, single parenting, God, faith, and church developed and grew strongly during this season of sessions with Steve.

****

Josh finished his letter to his father, stood up, and then paced around the room while he read it out loud to make sure it conveyed what he wanted it to say. He was pleased with his words but still didn't know if his dad would even read it, let alone respond. Oh well, that wasn't the intent or the purpose of the letter. The process couldn't have anything to do with a result, or it wouldn't help Josh continue to grow in authentic expression and relationships free of co-dependency and manipulation – something foreign to most addicts.

Josh grabbed his wallet out of his duffel bag and pulled out his picture of Heather and Henry and stared at it for a long time. Tomorrow he would write his letter to each of them. Josh put the picture back in his wallet and slid it into his back pocket. He grabbed his Bible from the same bag and decided to read the first couple of chapters from the Gospels of Matthew and Luke. These were the two books of the Bible with the most details of the life of Jesus, fitting during the Christmas season. They also encouraged Josh because Jesus was also born into an impoverished family.

Around 8:30 p.m., Josh woke up and recognized he'd fallen asleep while reading. He was reenergized and hungry and decided to go for a walk. The church was a couple of miles from the town square, and it was pretty cold, but Josh was up for the brisk walk and wanted to be around people. He took his time to soak in the beauty of the nature around him and reached the diner around 9:15 p.m. He bought a paper from the machine, took a seat at a booth where he could watch the people walk by on the sidewalk, and ordered a piece of pie and a coffee. He sat quietly and peacefully, glad to be free and sober, and reflected on his last meetings with the career counselor before his discharge from rehab. It was pretty obvious in his scores and assessments Josh needed to be in a job where he could move and where he could serve others. The role must have structure and authority, but enough autonomy for his independence to flourish. Josh circled some potential jobs in the want ads. One was a sales job for security systems. Another was a management role at the YMCA, though he didn't really think he was qualified. None of them really excited him, but his attention was quickly diverted by the man who slid in the seat across from him. It was the fire chief.

"I thought it was you. Man, it's so good to see you. How long have you been back in Sugar Grove?"

"It is good to see you too, sir," Josh said humbly and happily. "I've been out of rehab for less than a week. I was messed up pretty bad, sir, and am so sorry for abandoning you and the men."

"Apology accepted, Josh. Jim Miller let me know you were safe and receiving treatment at a rehabilitation facility. I prayed for you while you were gone."

"Thanks so much," Josh said humbly. "I am so glad to be sober, and I also have a relationship with Jesus Christ now. He is my Lord and Savior, sir."

"Well, that is awesome to hear. 'Trust in the Lord with all your heart and lean not on your own understanding. In all your ways acknowledge Him, and He will direct your path,'" said the chief, quoting Proverbs 3: 5-6.

"That's one of my favorite verses also, sir."

"You looking for work?" the chief asked, glancing down at the paper.

"Yes, sir. Not sure what I want to do, but I know from the career counseling in rehab I need a job with activity, movement, and the opportunity to serve others."

"Are you going to apply for reinstatement?"

"You mean that I could?" Josh asked, stunned.

"Absolutely," the chief replied joyfully. "There may be some drug screenings required, AA meetings, and a conversation with your sponsor, but you were hands-down the best driver we've ever had and as brave and courageous as any fireman who's ever worked in Sugar Grove. We'd be overjoyed to have you back."

Josh couldn't help himself. The tears flowed freely down his cheeks, and he looked down at the newspaper, crumpled it up, and tossed it down to the side of him. "I will be there first thing Monday morning and fill out the paperwork, sir. I don't have access to a computer."

"That is great, Josh. I have to get back to my wife and kids, but it is so, so good to see you. You look healthy and happy. Merry Christmas, son."

"Merry Christmas to you, sir, and to your family." Josh stood and offered his hand to shake the chief's hand.

The chief moved his hand aside, grabbed Josh by the arm, and pulled him in for a strong embrace. It was only the third hug Josh had ever had from a man. The first was from his counselor at rehab, and the second was from Pastor Steve two days earlier. His response to each was the same. He cried and had a hard time letting go.

Chapter 17

Ryan woke up Christmas Eve around 6:00 a.m. emotionally drained. He wanted to sleep longer but couldn't. First, he was a morning person and usually couldn't sleep past 6:00 a.m. no matter when he went to bed the night before. Second, Buford was a morning dog, and as soon as he knew Ryan was awake, even just a little bit, he was out of his bed and in Ryan's, nuzzling and talking to his master. Ryan scratched Buford's belly with one hand and behind one of his ears with the other. After a satisfactory amount of attention, Buford jumped off the bed and began to twirl and look at Ryan with anticipation.

"OK, boy, go get your leash," Ryan commanded.

As soon as Ryan said "boy," Buford was gone. Ryan scurried out of bed, knowing he had to hustle, or Buford would be back and start barking, possibly waking up his mother. It was obvious Buford needed to get outside quickly today. He was almost ten, and his bladder was not nearly as strong as it had been when he was younger. Ryan brushed his teeth quickly, threw on his sweats, and was ready when Buford returned with the leash in his mouth. Becky's door was still closed, so Ryan and Buford were quiet on their way downstairs and into the kitchen. Ryan grabbed a muffin and a bottle of water, and they headed out the back deck door for their walk.

"Buford, I think we're definitely moving back to Sugar Grove. What do you think about that, old man?" Buford listened but didn't seem to be in the mood to talk this morning. It didn't stop Ryan.

"I am going to need to talk to George sooner than later," Ryan continued. George Ramirez was the chair of the Emerging board and a good friend. "I also meet John in a couple of hours, and I need to have some potential positions created for him and the other board members. I'll need to spend some time in Dad's office when we get back."

Buford seemed preoccupied and offered very little feedback. Ryan was not offended and stayed quiet for the remainder of the lap around the property. He did, however, for the first time in a long time, want to talk to the Lord. There was a lot to sort through, and he wanted the guidance of God in these monumental life decisions. As they came around the far side of the barn, he broke the silence with a reflection and summary of his prayer. "Christ Effortlessly Omniscient," Ryan said out loud to himself, recognizing how his choices in acronymic phrases had shifted this week. This one was about the Lord, and the last several were about the community around him and less about himself. Ryan decided to jog the last hundred yards, which perked Buford's playful spirit, and he lumbered alongside Ryan joyfully until they reach the front door.

****

Heather and Henry ate their annual Christmas Eve chocolate chip pancake breakfast. Heather decided not to invite Ryan so that she and Henry could keep some of their own traditions, and Henry didn't protest when she explained to him why Ryan wasn't there. They were both still glowing in post-victory celebration as they wolfed down the tasty, albeit unhealthy, meal.

"Mom, what are you going to do with the money from the Happy Henry's?" Henry asked through a mouthful of chocolate and syrup.

"All of it will go into your college fund," Heather said, smiling.

"What if I don't want to go to college?" Henry asked.

"Not an option," Heather replied, "but it's nothing we need to worry about yet since you haven't even started first grade yet."

"Gabby told me she might not go to high school or college."

"Oh really?" Heather smiled and awaited whatever humorous plan Gabby had not only orchestrated in her mind but already shared with Henry.

"Yes. She said professional skaters don't go to high school."

"Well, that is sometimes true," Heather confirmed, "but professional ice skaters have an even tougher schedule than most high schoolers. They practice for probably six or seven hours a day and then have to do their schoolwork on their own or with a tutor anyway."

"Wow," Henry exclaimed, "I don't think Gabby knows that. I better tell her. Are we going to the Christmas Eve service tonight?" he asked.

"Of course," Heather affirmed quickly.

"Are we going with Ryan or with Dad?" Henry asked cautiously.

"With Ryan and Gabby's family," Heather replied. Curious about his inquiry, she asked, "Do you want your dad to come?"

Henry hesitated a second, but then, when he sensed it was safe, replied in the affirmative, although he didn't look at his mom when he answered.

"Well," Heather said, a bit startled by Henry's desire, "I'll have to check with Ryan about that first."

"Thanks, Mom." Henry beamed and continued to devour his pancakes.

Heather tried to hide her nervous energy at Henry's request, but it definitely stirred her soul. A few minutes later they both were done, and Henry dropped an even bigger bombshell on her Christmas Eve expectations.

"Can I give Dad a present?" Henry asked while he put his plate in the dishwasher.

"Of course," Heather answered, unsurprised by the generous heart of her effervescent son.

Chapter 17

"What do you want to give him? An ornament or some North Pole popcorn?" Heather asked, trying to be equally enthusiastic.

"No," Henry said flatly. "I want to give him something special."

"What did you have in mind?"

"I want to give him the money from the Happy Henry's," Henry proclaimed dramatically. "Dad doesn't have any money, and the Happy Henry's are supposed to make people happy. Don't you think the money would make Dad happy?"

Heather had to brace herself on the sink counter, her heart overcome with emotion and punctured by the love of her son. The tears that followed were sprung from pride in her son but also her sinful pride – as she never considered giving the money away, and especially not to Josh.

"Come here, my wonderful son," Heather requested with her arms open.

Henry walked over and hugged his mother, who was now kneeling on the floor. "That is a wonderful idea, Henry. Nothing would share the love of Jesus with your daddy more than giving him the cookie money. I am so proud of you. We'll get a nice card and head over to the church today or tomorrow."

"I want to give it to him today, Mom," Henry exclaimed confidently now that he saw his mother was fine with his request.

"OK, baby, I'll get a hold of Pastor Steve in just a few minutes."

****

Ryan spent some time writing out possibilities for his future without strong conviction or passionate energy. He needed to talk with George to see what options might be available through Emerging. George's response would dictate his approach with John. Ryan had texted George at 8:00 to ask him if he could have a conversation with him sometime in the next few days.

He knew a Christmas Eve text would generate some urgency and it did. George texted immediately that he would make time in an hour, and at 9:00 a.m. sharp he FaceTimed Ryan. "What's up, CEO?" George asked playfully, his standard greeting to Ryan.

"Merry Christmas to you and the family." Ryan wanted to start with some pleasantries, but George didn't have time for small talk. His wife was already frustrated with his calling Ryan on Christmas Eve.

"You didn't text me on Christmas Eve to wish me a Merry Christmas, Ryan, so go ahead and tell me what's on your mind."

"Well, I know this will sound rash and impulsive, but I want to move back to Sugar Grove."

"Want to or will do?" George asked poignantly.

"I plan on moving back sometime soon, George, and my father left me controlling interest of the North Pole Candy Company. I don't even know if

Emerging will allow me to stay in my current role while I'm owner of another company."

"Wow," George said. "Congratulations. North Pole is an iconic Northern Minnesota company. I don't think our board will have any issue with your serving in both roles as long as your production at Emerging continues to be excellent, but I don't know for sure. I assume your ownership of North Pole does not include day-to-day executive oversight?"

"Not at this point it doesn't," Ryan acknowledged, "but I would like to spend most of my time in Sugar Grove, so I wanted to give you and the board time to decide whether you would consider a remote CEO."

"OK," George said pensively. "You sound firm on your desire to move home. I am tentatively willing to consider this, but, of course, the full board will need to discuss this after Christmas, and we will get back to you before the January 5th board meeting."

"Sounds good, George. I appreciate your time on Christmas Eve and your openness to consider this. As you probably would have guessed, I have put together some possible options and will email those to the board on Monday. And, to be fully transparent, I'm meeting with a few of the North Pole board members at 10:00 to discuss my ownership and the movements of the company. There is a good chance they will ask me to consider becoming their CEO, and I am open to that consideration."

"My goodness!" George exclaimed. "What happened to you in Sugar Grove this week?"

"It's a combination of things, but there is a woman involved – Heather Hayes, the woman I almost married seven years ago. She is now divorced, and we are dating."

"Now, it all makes sense," George laughed. "Nothing can change a man quicker than the love of a woman."

"You're right, George. I have been home for less than a week, and I feel like a totally different man. But, to be fair, it's just not Heather that has changed me. I have been such an obsessive executive the past few years I have failed to be anything else, and my life in the city is boring and absent of community. I love my team and we have a great culture at Emerging, but it's not enough anymore – or it's too much – one or the other, or both."

"I understand, Ryan. It definitely sounds like you've been doing some soul searching."

"That's an understatement. Thanks for your time. And have a Merry Christmas."

"You too, Ryan. We'll talk soon."

****

Heather called Pastor Steve around 8:30 a.m., and he was as moved by Henry's generosity as Heather was.

"What an amazing gesture by a little boy, the faith of a child," Pastor Steve commented. Once again, sermon illustrations were flowing this week for Steve.

"Henry wants to give the check to Josh today, Pastor."

"Alright, I think we should follow his lead and his heart. Let me run down to the church and see what Josh is doing today. He is probably painting again. I'll check with him and check with my wife and get back to you as soon as I can."

"OK, thanks, but don't tell him about the gift. I want Henry to surprise him."

"Of course. What a gift from God this will be for Josh."

****

Ryan arrived at Sugar Grove Country Club at 9:45 to be respectfully early, but it didn't matter; John and the two additional North Pole Board members, Timothy Peterson and Ted Chambers, were already eating brunch. John saw Ryan almost immediately and waved him over to join them at the table. A plate was already prepared for him with some eggs, bacon, and hash browns. In addition, a glass of orange juice and a black coffee had already been poured. John was a planner, an organizer, and was also the best prosecuting attorney in the county. He thought of everything and everybody but was not absent of ego or ambition. He was wise enough to use his personal capital only when it was necessary. Otherwise, he led by influence, experience, credibility, and collaborative alliances and networking. Jim and John had been close friends, and Ryan was a bit intimidated by their relationship. He knew that John might have known his father better than Ryan had.

The men all stood to meet Ryan when he reached the table. Ryan shook hands firmly and expressed his sincere appreciation for the meeting. He guessed correctly the men would be dressed business casual and had strategically dressed more formally. This was not an official interview, but Ryan knew it might as well be; and, if nothing else, this was the first meeting for the new owner of North Pole with three of the most important, most influential, and wealthiest board members. Ryan wore a Burberry suit from London, but without the tie. It made the statement Ryan wanted it to, for Ted recognized the brand.

Conversation during the meal was limited to John's law practice, the Dow Jones, and the Sugar Grove real estate market. Ryan listened more than he talked and felt comfortable with the men, even though they were all 25 years older than he. He also made mental notes of some of the new subdivisions sprouting up between Sugar Grove and the Twin Cities in case he ended up in a hybrid relationship with both companies and needed to be close to both. Pine Bluff was the development he wanted to investigate further, with 5,000-square foot homes starting for $800,000. It sounded ideal to Ryan, but he wondered if Heather wanted to live in that kind of home. And would Henry be willing to change neighborhoods if it meant being further away from Gabby? Ryan must have been lost in thought because John brought him back into the present with a very direct statement.

"Ryan, we asked you to join us this morning, so we could get an understanding of what you intend to do as owner of North Pole." John's tone and tenor of communication had shifted into courtroom presentation. "After your profound disclosure last night, it seems obvious to us you have experienced a change of heart regarding North Pole and Sugar Grove."

"Yes sir, I have," Ryan affirmed.

"It also seems," John continued sharply, but with a smile, "that your relationship with Vice President Hayes has also redeveloped quite quickly."

"Yes, sir, that is also correct."

Chapter 17

Like a skilled litigation lawyer, John built the narrative to secure his position and to lead Ryan into confession. "As you also know, Ryan, our CEO position is open and set to be released for a national search next week. Your father will never be replaced, but we do need a new executive leader at North Pole."

"Yes, sir, I am aware of that opening," Ryan replied, not willing to reveal his hand just yet, and allowed John to carry the conversation.

"We also recognize your accomplishments and achievements at Emerging Enterprises are nothing short of remarkable." Ryan knew John would not flatter and likely had assistants thoroughly research Ryan and Emerging. He wondered how many of John's paralegals spent part of their Christmas break investigating his career. "We also read this week of Emerging's newest and strongest merger. Congratulations, Ryan. To secure that deal amidst the holiday season and the death and memorial of your father is quite impressive."

"Thank you, sir. Our entire leadership team is responsible for that accomplishment. It was quite a blessing, and there may be more residual movements coming."

"I'd love to hear more, but I am sure you are not at liberty to reveal. What we would like to know, however, is if you have thought through the possibility of applying for the CEO position at North Pole?"

Ryan leaned forward in his chair and made sure to make eye contact with each of the men before he started. Now it was his turn to change his style of communication, and he talked louder and more emphatically. "Gentlemen, I have indeed thought and prayed about this position. I actually talked with the chair of Emerging's board this morning and told him I was meeting with you." He paused for dramatic effect before he continued. "I am committed to moving back to Sugar Grove as soon as possible." Ryan waited for a response, but there was none; they did not seem surprised. "Our Emerging chair is convening virtually with our board on the 26th to ask them if they are willing to consider a remote CEO. I honestly don't know what they will determine, but if they are not comfortable with the change in my residence, then I will most likely submit my resignation. They also may not be comfortable with a CEO who owns another company not affiliated with them. I'll know soon, but, either way, I will give them time to replace me and will stay long enough to stabilize the internal processes during the transition. They have been very good to me."

This time it was Ted who spoke. "If I were the chair of Emerging's board, I would work with you remotely, but I would assume you would lose intensity and passion for the company when you were away from the people."

"You are probably right, Ted." Ryan thought of his leaving ritual, last performed a week ago, and how even when the office was noisy and distracting it was still full of energy. "I would be willing to open a new office for Emerging in Sugar Grove and bring some of my staff and their families with me. The new merger would allow us the flexibility to create a new office without a major loss in revenue the first few years."

Ted nodded in affirmation. "Interesting idea, Ryan. It would be great to have a new business in town. Have you thought of a location?"

"Of course," Ryan said confidently, though he had only thought of a few places last night on the way home. "The old Catholic school, St Rita's, is available. I think it could be renovated in a historic, but progressive manner. We could also refurbish the gym and cafeteria for some community service ventures."

"Also, a great idea," Tim chimed in. "There is talk of the dioceses razing the building and selling off the property, so you might want to contact your realtor sooner than later."

"Thanks for the information," Ryan replied, gaining excitement and vision for what could happen.

John shifted the discussion back to North Pole. "My son Robert is interviewing for the CEO role on Monday, Ryan. He is also a gifted leader."

"I agree, John. And if I am still around next week, it will be good to see him. Robert would be a fantastic CEO for North Pole, but if I did apply and you hired me, how would we handle Heather and her VP position? That would certainly be against company policy."

"We would approach that issue if and when we had to," John answered strongly. "It would be a good problem to solve if we had two great leaders working for North Pole who had a pre-existing relationship prior to their employment together. I am sure we could work through those legal matters with the board and reach some appropriate conclusions." There was some awkward silence for a minute, and Ryan did not try to fill the space. He sensed something was still unsaid, and he was right. John finally continued, "And there is one more revelation we want to share before you return home."

Chapter 18

Henry was out of his seat belt and almost out the door before Heather pulled into the parking spot closest to the church entrance, the first one available next to the handicap spaces. He was so excited to see his dad and to give him his present.

"Wait a second, Honey," Heather exclaimed. She could tell Henry was on warp speed. "Let's grab some of your father's things from the storage unit I have in the trunk."

"OK," Henry said, obviously disappointed. He fidgeted up and down with the zipper of his coat as he tried to remain patient. Heather opened the trunk and gathered some clothes and a box. She also handed Henry a small bag to carry full of fireman uniforms Josh had left behind.

"Can I give it to him right away?" Henry wondered aloud.

"The bag, yes. The card, no. Remember how we practiced it?" Heather reminded him.

"Oh yeah. Pastor Steve will talk first. We will sit down together and ask Dad how he is doing, and then we give him the card and wish him a Merry Christmas."

"That's right. I see Pastor Steve at the door, so let's hustle. It's cold."

Henry needed no more encouragement and sprinted up the sidewalk to meet the pastor while Heather quickly followed.

After a hug, Pastor Steve ushered them into his office where Josh was already seated on the love seat. He had two envelopes in his hands and looked nervous. Henry broke the tension by dropping the bag by his dad and jumping into his arms. Josh wasn't quite ready, and Henry almost kneed Josh in the face. The startled physicality of the greeting was a tension-reducer for Josh and the others in the room.

Chapter 18

Steve and Heather watched the aggressive embrace before they sat in the two seats across the table from Josh. After an appropriate amount of bear-cub wrestling, Josh instructed Henry to take the only other empty chair situated next to him. Steve opened the gathering with a quick prayer and some ground rules for interaction and then turned the floor immediately over to Henry. Henry could barely stay seated for the energy and excitement in his body. He pulled out a folded envelope from one side of his coat and a zip-lock bag of Happy Henry's from his other coat pocket and gave them both to Josh.

"Dad, we hope you are doing well. Merry Christmas. Mom and I decided to give you a Christmas present, and I also packed you some of my cookies." Henry said the three memorized statements so quickly it was hard to decipher what was said, and he almost threw the card and cookies at his father.

"This is for me?" Josh asked Henry, for clarification, and Henry nodded his head aggressively and affirmatively.

"Thanks, Henry," Josh said with a huge smile. "And thank you, Heather." Josh glanced at Heather warmly and a bit shyly.

Josh set the cookies on the table and opened the envelope. The check inside fell to the ground. Startled and surprised, Josh retrieved the check and glanced at the amount as he brought it back to his chest. He stopped moving and tears welled up in his eyes. Eventually he turned to Heather as he shook his head side to side.

"This is an amazing gift and gesture, but I can't accept this, Heather."

Henry was ready for this defense and did not wait for his mother to respond.

"Dad, that is the money from the North Pole Cookie Contest. Mom and I won and those are the cookies in your bag – the Happy Henry's. They are supposed to make people happy, and we wanted you to be happy this Christmas."

Josh looked over at Henry and saw the joy in his son's eyes and his ear-to-ear smile and couldn't contain the tears any longer. He sank back into his chair and used the envelope to shade his face. Henry was not sure what to do next, so he looked over at his mother.

After a couple of seconds of silence, Heather shared more.

"Josh," Heather said, waiting for Josh to look at her. When he did, she continued. "This gift was Henry's idea, and we hope this money blesses your new start in Sugar Grove."

Josh nodded thankfully and then invited Henry back to his lap by opening his arms wide. Henry obliged and gave his dad another enormous hug.

This time it was Josh's turn to bless. "Henry, this is the best Christmas present I have ever received, and it makes it even more special that it was your idea. And really, this Christmas is the best Christmas ever, just seeing you and being with you again. I don't have a physical gift for you, but I do have a card."

"Awesome!" Henry declared as Josh gave him the card. Henry ripped it open and had to give it to his mother to read. Heather read it out loud. Josh made the words and the length fitting for a five-year-old.

Merry Christmas, Henry! I love you and I will never leave you again! You are the best gift God has ever given me. Love, Dad.

The words prompted another long hug between father and son, and Heather grabbed her Kleenex from her coat pocket. She had come prepared. Steve kept quiet and simply observed the love and grace.

Josh wasn't done. "Heather, I have a card for you also." Josh moved Henry back to his chair and slid the envelope across the coffee table. Heather was so nervous she felt faint, and her hands trembled as she leaned forward to retrieve the envelope without looking at Josh.

"Thank you," she offered in a whisper, sitting back in her chair. "If it is OK with everybody, I want to read my card to myself first."

No one said a word, so she carefully opened the seal, then the card, and unfolded the letter inside.

Dearest Heather, words can never describe how truly sorry I am for failing you as a man, a husband, and as a father. I abandoned you and Henry, and it was a shameful and despicable act. Please forgive me and accept my most profound apologies. I beg for your mercy and grace yet again – the same grace Jesus gave to me and that you showed me in our marriage.

Heather stopped to glance at Pastor Steve first and then quickly at Josh who pensively watched in hopeful anticipation. She started to visibly shake but continued.

You are an amazingly beautiful, kind, gracious, and gifted woman, and I was the luckiest man in the world to meet you during the most traumatic time of your life. Instead of loving you through the grieving, I used you for my own addiction.

Heather shifted in her chair uncomfortably and wondered how much more her heart could handle. She had never received a written card from Josh before, so this well-crafted confession was challenging on multiple levels. She ventured ahead, though she gasped a few times, holding back the flood of emotions that tried to surface.

I am not using drugs as an excuse, but you never knew the true me because I *didn't know the true me. I am just discovering him now, but I promise on my new life, and with my Savior as my accountability and my witness, to be a committed and consistent father to Henry and to follow all your boundaries and guidelines for relationship. Please receive the following declaration in the right spirit. I love you with all my heart, soul, mind, and strength, and I will love you for eternity. It was your love that I thought of when I was alone in the streets. It was your love I remembered when I was in rehabilitation. It was your love that saved me until I learned that only Jesus can save me, that His life, death, and resurrection paid the penalty for my sins, and that whoever believes in Him in their heart and confesses Him as Lord with their mouth is saved! The love of Jesus now saves me. The love of Jesus now motivates me. The love of Jesus now gives me purpose. The love of Jesus will allow me to be a great father to Henry and a great friend to you. In the name of the Father, and the Son, and the Holy Spirit – I love you, Josh.*

Heather folded the letter carefully, placed it back in the card, looked for somewhere to place it, and eventually handed it to Pastor Steve. It was too intense and too soul provoking to hold onto now, though she wanted to keep it. She had no idea what to say or do next. After a few awkward seconds, she attempted a grateful response.

"Thank you" was all she could manage before the emotional tsunami swept through her soul, into her heart, and out of her lungs and mouth. She excused herself as she spun out of her chair, frantically opened the door, and lunged out of the office. She ran down the hallway as the weeping started, made it into the sanctuary, but collapsed in the aisle well before the stage. Her body heaved in contorted spasms, and she began to wail in a cathartic rhythm, seven years of stored grieving finally released to the Lord.

The three men in the office could hear Heather sobbing, and Henry left his chair to be comforted by his father. "What is wrong with Mommy?" Henry asked Josh as his tears also began to flow.

"I don't know for sure, Henry, but I told her how sorry I was, and I told her how much Jesus loves me and how much I love her," Josh said unapologetically.

"Then why is she crying so hard and so loud?" Henry asked quite frightened by his mother's response.

"Because I should have told her these things when we were married and because I apologized to her for being a terrible husband and father. Your mom is a strong woman who had to go through a lot of heartache because of me."

Henry curled into his father's strong arms and tried to understand.

Steve finally spoke. "I am going to go check on Heather."

"OK," Josh said for both of them. "We'll stay here."

"That's probably a good idea," Steve said a little concerned. "I don't know how long we'll be, so if you guys need to go to the youth room or to the gym, that's fine. We'll come find you wherever you guys end up."

****

John spoke with the tone of a judge. Many in the county thought John would have been an excellent one, but he never pursued it because of his love for litigation. "Ryan, we don't want you to apply for the CEO position of North Pole." Ryan was taken back by this pronouncement but waited for the explanation before he responded. John assumed this reaction and let it marinate for a moment before he continued. "The board is pretty confident in my son as our new CEO, and with that upcoming appointment, I will resign as a board member due to the conflict of interest." Ryan thought this ironic, for just a couple of minutes earlier, John had told Ryan not to worry about his and Heather's relationship being a similar possible breach of ethics, but now was not the time to comment on that inconsistency. "We don't want you to apply as CEO," John continued with authority, "because we want you to be the President of North Pole." John let the weight of the consideration linger with a whimsical smile. Ryan continued a stoic demeanor though his heart began to pound. John continued, "The president role has been vacant at North Pole since your grandfather retired in 1996, and we think his grandson is the next Miller to fulfill the role."

Chapter 18

Ryan was honored and a bit shocked by this proposal, which had not been on his radar as an option. He sat back in his chair to let the opportunity register further. Then, like a rushing wind, the message from his father to Pastor Steve about the conflict behind his grandfather's presidency and his father's appointment as CEO crashed into his conscious. This is what his dad had foreseen. This is why his father had given the letter to Pastor Steve, something Ryan still didn't have in his possession. Ryan smirked and shook his head slowly side to side, which confused John. "Does this mean you are not interested in the president role?" John asked, his confident tone no longer audible.

Ryan finally reentered the present. "No, no, I am sorry, John. I am very interested. I was shaking my head because my dad shared with Pastor Steve about the turmoil and tension around the North Pole CEO role 25 years ago and how that led to the creation of the president position. Pastor just told me about the resignation earlier this week and said Dad wanted me to know about it after the funeral. As always, Dad was thinking ahead, preparing me for my future whether I wanted to be prepared or not."

"Ah, yes," John concurred. "I was not on the board then, but I remember how angry and frustrated your father was. The board made the right decision, however. Joe was a fantastic president, and Jim was a great CEO. We have thought about the same kind of roles at North Pole for years, but the right people never surfaced before you and Robert both expressed interest this month. Your father, by the way, was not aware of this discussion prior to his coma, Ryan." John let that news saturate for all of them to consider. "God works in mysterious ways, but it took your dad's death to bring new life and movement to this company, and he must have anticipated your desire to return one day. After your speech at the cookie contest, the board knew you were ready, and you were the right man to consider for this role." John took an envelope out of his suit pocket and slid it across the table to Ryan. "Here are some preliminary responsibilities and numbers to start the negotiation process and to help you compare to your package at Emerging."

Ryan did not open the envelope and slipped it into his suit pocket. He wanted to look at the preliminary offer in privacy and discuss with Buford and Heather before he communicated back with them. "Thank you, men, for your faith and belief in me despite my years of ignoring and disregarding my father and North Pole. If I may have a few days to ponder and pray about this, I would greatly appreciate it."

"Of course," John assured him.

"Thank you. It really is a great honor to be considered for this position. I will also want to discuss how my stake as owner would coincide with the president role and how my relationship with Heather would be considered. She needs to be able to retain her position or I am not interested. Does she know anything about this possibility?"

"We don't believe Heather knows about the president position or about my son being a strong candidate for the CEO role. We did not discuss the new executive structure with any of the leadership team during the end-of-year evaluations and review. The board carried this function through this year due to your dad's condition. And of course, Heather's role, if your relationship continued into your tenure as president, would not be jeopardized or altered."

"Good," Ryan affirmed. "I think it's fair. Did you consider Heather or any of the other vice presidents for the position?"

"We did not, Ryan. As you well know, CEO and president positions are unique and difficult to fill. During the review meetings, when we discussed the likely open CEO role for next year, none of the VP's expressed interest. They were content with their current roles."

"May I have your permission to discuss this with my mother and Heather prior to the leadership team's learning of the possibility? Ryan asked tentatively. "I know this puts the board in an awkward situation."

The men looked at each other inquisitively, and John sensed the need for communication. "Ryan, would you excuse yourself for ten minutes so we can discuss this? Please head over to the gift shop and pick something out for you and your mother on behalf of the board for Christmas."

"No problem," Ryan replied. "I will be glad to find a gift for my mom." Ryan was glad to get his mother something, but he knew John, not the board, would pay for the gift and Ryan needed to buy something to affirm John's benevolence.

Chapter 19

Josh and Henry sat in Pastor Steve's office for 20 minutes before they got really bored and headed down to the freshly painted youth room. Steve gave Heather plenty of space and stayed outside the sanctuary where he could see her, but not interrupt her, until Heather's sobs turned into whimpers. Steve did not want to join her too quickly and stifle the healing. After Heather stood up and made her way toward the stage, Steve slipped in the back door.

"Do you need anything?" he asked gently

"A glass of water, some tissues, and an update on Henry," she responded.

Steve went to the church kitchen down the hall and quickly returned with the water and tissues and told her Josh and Henry had gone to the youth room. He sat with Heather on the stage stairs for another 15 minutes to process through the mourning. After Steve prayed for her, Heather glanced at her phone and saw it was 9:30. They had plenty of time to get to Tucker's hockey game, which she had promised Henry and Gabby they would attend. She gave Pastor Steve a warm hug and they walked together to find Henry.

Josh and Henry were playing cards in the youth room. Henry wanted to play his Nintendo, but Josh was not sure he was allowed, so he steered Henry toward some cards. He taught him Crazy 8's, and Henry loved the game, especially since he throttled his father handedly. Josh then taught Henry War, which he knew would take enough time to wait out Heather and Steve. Henry was just about ready to defeat Josh at War, as well, when Heather and Steve walked into the room.

"How are you two doing?" Heather asked lightly. She looked much better now, and both of them were eased by her demeanor.

Chapter 19

"I am about ready to win, Mom," Henry declared triumphantly. Josh nodded his head slowly up and down in concession and admission.

"I taught Henry Crazy 8's, and he beat me three times in a row. Then I taught him War, and he's about ready to beat me in this game also," Josh added. "My son is a natural at cards."

Henry was ecstatic and finished Josh off with just three more card challenges as Steve and Heather watched the young victor celebrate his glorious win over his father.

"We need to leave soon, Henry, if we are going to make Tucker's hockey game," Heather reminded him. "Gabby is probably already at the rink."

"Oh yeah!" Henry shrieked excitedly. "Can Dad come?" Before Heather could answer, Henry turned to ask his father.

"Do you want to come watch Tucker play hockey? He is really good, and his team wins most of the time. Gabby is going to be there, too."

Josh looked at Heather before even offering a nonverbal clue. She smiled and gave a slight shoulder shrug and gentle affirmative nod, so Josh knew it was permissible. "Absolutely, Henry! I'd love to come to the game and hang out with you some more," Josh said with as much joy in his voice as Henry had displayed when extending the invitation.

"Let's go!" Henry shouted, turning to his mother and asking for his coat.

"Our coats are back in Pastor's office, Henry."

"OK. Come on, Dad. We need to go. I don't want to be late." Then Henry grabbed Josh's hand with one hand and his mother's hand with the other, and down the hall they went. Heather looked over her shoulder, a bit bewildered, at Steve. Steve caught her eyes and smiled. They waited in the hall while Steve brought their coats out to them. Henry was swinging back and forth in his parents' arms, fully enjoying the unity he had been without for over a year.

****

Ryan left the country club and briskly walked to his Corvette. There was a sharp northwest wind. Snow was on the way. His mind raced, and he desperately wanted to see and talk to Heather. His emotions were somewhere between exhilaration, panic, and anticipation. He checked his phone – almost 11:00. If he hustled, he could probably catch some of the third period of Tucker's game at North Pole. He texted his mother and Heather that he was on his way. His mom answered right away. The second period was almost over and Tucker's team was winning 2-1. Heather simply responded with a thumbs up.

The country club was on the other side of town, so when Ryan pulled into North Pole he could see there was only 7:36 on the game clock, and the score was tied at 2 in the third and final period. Parking was tight, so by the time he found a safe space for his Corvette and made his way to the rink gate, there was only 5:15 left. They didn't charge him an entry fee, so he could watch the end of the game for free, but Ryan handed the ticket table boy some cash anyway. He scanned the crowd for his family, but it was packed, and everybody was bundled up, so he didn't see them until Jennifer spotted him and stood up to wave him over. Ryan took a few steps in that direction and then noticed Heather, Henry, and Josh in the front row, with Jennifer, his mother, Gabe, and Gabby one row above them. Ryan slowed his pace for a moment as he considered the seating arrangement and the presence of Josh. There was room beside Heather to squeeze in, but Ryan didn't feel comfortable being in the same row with the three of them. He said hello quickly and stepped past Heather into the row with his sister.

Chapter 19

Regulation ended at two goals apiece, necessitating a five-minute overtime period of only four-on-four skating, down from the regular five players skating against five players in the regulation time periods. The teams switched ends to defend, and there was a brief five-minute intermission so the coaches could restructure their line-ups with the new variables in play. This was just long enough for a strange and awkward conversation to take place, which Heather initiated when she turned around to face Ryan and Jennifer.

"How did the meeting go with John and the board members?" she asked.

"It went really well. They shared some pretty significant opportunities for me and for the company," Ryan replied.

"Like what?" Jennifer asked before Heather could.

"I am not at liberty to share yet," Ryan said a bit coldly. This bothered both women, and Ryan knew this wouldn't have a good ending.

"What could be so secretive that you can't share it with your sister and your girlfriend, who also works at the company?" Jennifer said on behalf of both ladies.

"Something that hasn't been communicated even to the full board yet," Ryan said directly, more annoyed with his sister for pressing him than with the reality of the issue.

"Well, that seems weird and disappointing," Heather said sadly.

"Kind of like this seating arrangement," Ryan responded with an edge and motioned toward Josh and Henry.

Heather bent closer to Ryan and Jennifer before whispering that Henry wanted Josh to come to the game.

Chapter 19

"Uncle Ryan," Henry interjected before Ryan could offer a rebuttal, "isn't this a great game? My dad came to watch with me. Isn't that cool?"

Ryan couldn't deny Henry's enthusiasm for his father or the game and agreed with Henry on both points. He turned to Heather again and leaned in toward her. "I really need to talk to you sometime today, as soon as possible, and alone."

"OK," Heather said firmly. She didn't like Ryan's tone and was unsure of his spirit at the moment. "I'll call you later today after we drop Josh back off at the church."

"You rode together?" Ryan asked, irritated.

"Henry orchestrated the whole thing," Heather explained as the head official blew the whistle to announce the start of overtime. Heather turned around dejected.

Ryan tried to stay present and cheer on his nephew, but his mind raced. Jennifer sensed his mental state and grabbed his arm and whispered in his ear, "What's up with the attitude?"

Ryan leaned in close to stay quiet and retorted, "What's up with Josh being here?"

Jennifer ended the interchange with the truth that would define and determine Ryan's next two days and maybe his entire future: "He's Henry's father."

****

The game ended in a tie, but there were two more games in the pool-play portion of the tournament, so Tucker's team could easily still advance to the playoffs on Monday and Tuesday, even with the tie. Tucker had played an outstanding game, scoring scored both his team's goals, but, of course, Ryan had missed them. After the coach dismissed his team, Tucker skated over to see his family, who had stayed in their corner of the rink. Gabe and Jennifer gave Tucker a hug, and Henry and Gabby clapped for their hockey star. Ryan moved down to the ice to talk to Tucker, but Josh began to talk with Tucker first.

"Great stick handling," Josh offered.

"Thanks, sir," Tucker responded.

"You can call me Josh, Tucker."

"OK," Tucker said.

"I thought your goals were both scored because of fantastic positioning. Your net presence in the offensive zone was excellent. You covered a ton of ground also on your forechecking." Josh and his brothers knew hockey – as everyone in Minnesota knew hockey – even if it was not a sport he had played competitively.

"Thanks," Tucker answered surprised by Josh's knowledge. "Our game plan was to try and control the neutral zone, so we could get scoring chances in transition or during shift changes.

"I think you guys did that well," Josh responded. "And your face offs were great. I think you won at least six of the nine you took."

"That's right," Tucker said, surprised. "That's what the stat sheet said. Uncle Ryan, I saw you come in toward the end of the game. Sorry you missed my goals."

"Me too," Ryan said. "I should be able to make tonight's game, so put a couple more biscuits in the basket tonight."

"I'll try," Tucker quipped. "Mom, can we get something to eat? I'm starving."

"Sure," Jennifer said.

"Why don't we order pizza and come back to my house?" Becky offered.

"Sounds great to me," Tucker responded.

"Me, too," Henry exclaimed.

"Yeah," Gabby piped in, "a party at Grandma's!"

Chapter 19

"Can my dad come also?" Henry asked Becky.

"Of course, he can," Becky replied. "It's Christmas Eve. Everyone needs to be with family. We can all go to church together after the second game."

Josh looked up at Becky with great warmth and appreciation. "Thank you, ma'am," Josh said humbly and respectfully.

"My pleasure," Becky replied, giving Josh a gentle touch on his shoulder.

Ryan clenched his teeth and kept his mouth shut. Heather could sense his frustration and didn't know what to do or say to make it better, so she kept quiet. Everyone proceeded to their cars and Ryan asked Becky to ride with him and told the others they would pick up the pizza and bring it home. As soon as they pulled out of the North Pole property, Ryan unloaded on his mother.

"I don't know if I can do this, Mom. Since Josh has come back, I haven't been with Heather hardly at all."

"Of course, you can, Honey. If you love the woman, you love what comes with the woman."

"But another man comes with the woman!"

"Yes, he does. And so does a child. But there is no way Heather can separate herself from Josh when Henry so desperately needs his father. Are you threatened by Josh?"

"Not with Heather, I don't think, but with Henry, yes. I honestly hoped I would get to be Henry's father figure. Now, he doesn't need me."

"That's nonsense, Honey. Every young child, and especially young boys, can use multiple father figures. This is all brand new. Josh has only been back for a few days. It's going to take time to figure these new relationships out."

Chapter 19

"I don't have time, Mom. John and the board offered me the President position at North Pole today. I need to decide fairly quickly whether I want to pursue the role and Heather is one of the primary reasons I would do so, but she doesn't even know I own the company, let alone that I could be her boss. This is getting really messy."

"Life is always messy, Ryan. It's how we handle the mess that determines our character."

"Very true, but some messes we can choose to be a part of, and others we can choose to avoid," Ryan retorted.

"Well said," Becky agreed, "but the mess with Heather is not going away anytime soon, so you'll have to decide, again, whether she is worth the messy investment of your heart and soul. I think she is. Some messes are beautiful."

"If Josh weren't around, I would completely agree. With Josh always going to be a part of Heather and Henry, I am not so sure I am wanted or needed." Ryan turned into the Pizza Palace parking lot, and he and Becky went in and picked up the food Jennifer had ordered.

****

They arrived home with three pizzas, two cups of breadsticks, 20 chicken wings, some cheese fries, and a couple of two liters of Coke. Ryan also ordered some dessert sticks for the kids, even though there was still some ice cream cake left over from the snowman contest victory. Jennifer had set the table, and all were seated, awaiting their food. Both heads of the table were open for Ryan and Becky. One was strategically placed next to a space near Heather. Henry and Josh were on the other side of her with Josh's seat next to where Becky would sit. Gabe's family was on the other side of the table. Ryan made appreciative eye contact with Jennifer as he carried the food to the island. Josh immediately got up from the table and took the two liters from Becky before Gabe could move to help. Josh poured everyone's drinks while Becky spread the food buffet-style on the island counter before asking Ryan to pray over the meal. Ryan obliged, even though he wasn't in a praying mood, which, of course, was probably why his mother asked him. His prayer thanked God for all His generous blessings, especially the birth of His Son Jesus.

They enjoyed their meal together, during which Josh told some riveting stories from his time training for MMA fights and from emergency calls in his previous tenure with the Sugar Grove Fire Department. Tucker and Henry were spellbound by the courageous stories, and the whole table was truly enthralled. Josh was a marvelous storyteller, appropriately exaggerating side details to build the plot and tension. He also shared the news of his interview and application process on Monday. Becky gushed over his opportunity, and he blushed. Gabe asked Josh where he was going to live, and Josh told him he didn't know yet, but he had received a Christmas gift that would afford him a renter's deposit for a nice apartment or condominium near the station.

"Mom and I gave Dad the gift," Henry declared unashamedly. "We gave him the Happy Henry's money from the cookie contest."

Everyone looked at each other in awe. "You did?" Becky responded, with joy and surprise. Heather and Henry both nodded. "That is so wonderful."

"It sure was, ma'am, the best Christmas gift I have ever received," Josh admitted.

"We wanted Daddy to be happy," Henry said proudly, "and Happy Henry's make people happy!"

Everyone looked at Heather. "It was Henry's idea," she acknowledged. "I am so proud of his generosity and a little ashamed that I did not think of it first."

Chapter 19

"Wow!" Jennifer exclaimed. "Henry, that is such a cool gift for your dad."

"Mom," Gabby chimed in, seeing how happy everyone was and wanting to join the celebration, "Can we give Mr. Josh some money also?"

Gabe spoke up first, "We sure can, Honey. That's an awesome idea. Why don't you and Henry go out next week with Josh and pick out some furniture for his new place?"

"And I am going to buy Josh a bedroom set," Becky announced, joining in the fun.

Josh was completely overwhelmed with this outpouring of love, and tears streamed down his face. Ryan watched the ordeal, unmoved by the showing of hospitality and generosity from his family until he saw the sincerity in Josh's response. But in the spirit of his father, who believed in Josh during his worst days, Ryan knew he must follow that example and bless the new man Josh was becoming. Ryan had to fight back his own tears as he stood up to command attention.

"Family, may I have your attention for a moment. Josh, my father loved you and believed in you when, frankly, not many people did. He saw a man who needed a second chance, a man who deserved grace and mercy. As executor of his estate, I know I honor the life of Jim Miller by helping you establish your new life in Christ and your new life in Sugar Grove. Therefore, next week, you may pick out a new truck as a Christmas gift from the Miller estate. My mother will help you with the paperwork and the check when I am back in the Twin Cities."

Before Ryan was even done with his proclamation, Josh was out of his seat and embraced Ryan in a bear hug that nearly took the wind out of Ryan. After a couple of violent slaps on the back that rattled Ryan's teeth, it was Josh's turn to address the family. He did so by turning around, but without letting go of Ryan as he kept one of his arms around Ryan's shoulders. "Thank you so much. This family has been used by the Lord to save my life, each and every one of you. Lots of people talk about loving others as Christ loved us, but this family is doing it and has been doing it for over a year and a half. I can't ever repay you for this generosity, but, if you allow me to, I will repay you with living a life similar to yours – giving, loving, helping, serving. Volunteering at the church. Helping to coach Henry and Tucker's teams. Helping Becky around this house on maintenance or projects. I have my life back and I now want to give that life away just like Jesus did. And, if you allow it, I will always be a part of this family." No one responded right away as Josh made his way back to his seat and so did Ryan.

"That was beautiful, Josh," Becky affirmed as she stood at her place. "And, of course, you are a part of this family. And if you need a place to stay until you find the condo or apartment you want, then please stay in our guest room here at the house."

"That would be fantastic," Josh replied. "I am thankful for the church allowing me to stay there, but it feels a bit strange living in a big church."

"It's settled then," Becky concluded. "Since we are all going to the Christmas Eve service at church tonight anyway, we will pick up your belongings and bring you back home when it's over."

Ryan reached under the table and grabbed Heather's hand. She squeezed his back. He leaned over to ask, "Can we steal away for a little bit? I really need to talk with you."

"Sounds wonderful," Heather replied, and they quietly excused themselves from the table.

Chapter 20

Ryan and Heather made their way to the living room to talk. Buford was the only other living creature in the room for this intimate and critical communication. He nestled against Heather's leg and, because she gave him affection, he curled up beside her on the floor and laid his head on her foot.

Ryan sat directly on the couch opposite Heather and leaned forward to begin a semi-rehearsed speech. "I have several things I need to share with you, including what John and the North Pole board offered me today. I received permission to share this news with you and my mother, but no one else, thus the short reply I gave at the game earlier."

"Ah, makes sense," Heather offered nervously. "You had a strange vibe at the game, so I was a bit irritated with your response. I've worked at North Pole for almost a decade, and it appeared as if they gave you special information when you haven't even agreed to work there yet. It seemed a bit unfair."

"Understood, and I'll explain that in a minute. I was irritated because I didn't know Josh was going to be there, and it felt I was intruding on your family, as if I'm the outsider now that he's back."

"I assumed you were annoyed, and I'm sorry about that," Heather agreed. "Henry's desire to be with his dad is constant, and it's really hard not to allow them time together as much as possible."

"I totally understand, and I am genuinely happy for Henry. Unless Josh is completely duping us, it seems like he is a good guy. I don't know how much he has changed, but I can see why you married him."

Heather shook her head back and forth, which confused Ryan at first, but her explanation clarified the nonverbal response. "Josh is a totally different person now. He has been transformed by the power of Christ. There is no other way to describe it. His joy. His emotionality. His kindness and gentleness. None of those traits were there before. The Josh you are getting to know is not a Josh that I know, either."

"Well, praise the Lord." Ryan surprised himself with his response. He had heard Pastor Steve give God the praise for life events so many times it must have moved into his new vernacular. "I am truly glad for him, but it really *has* complicated our relationship. You were married to him for seven years. He's Henry's dad." He paused thinking about the disclosure. "I hate to admit this, but I am jealous of his bond with Henry and his history with you. He is also a really good looking, strong, tough dude."

Ryan's acknowledgement of his jealousy softened Heather for a minute. "I understand that, Ryan, and his changed heart makes it much tougher to keep him away from Henry, which means he is also around me." Ryan noticed she didn't comment on his looks or their former relationship. This omission changed his disclosure to defense.

"I don't know how to deal with all that right now. I feel like I have to compete with Josh, and that stinks." Ryan needed to say more about it but put that on hold for a moment to talk about North Pole before everyone came back home. "The Josh stuff is important, but it's not the main reason I need to talk to you today."

"You have certainly piqued my interest now," Heather replied, leaning forward in her seat, glad to move off Josh and Henry at the moment.

"I should have told you this right away, so I apologize for keeping this information away from you for even a couple of days. I found out when I was sifting through my dad's files that he left me controlling interest of North Pole." Ryan had a big smile on his face and was excited to finally reveal this truth to Heather.

Chapter 20

Heather sat back in the couch to digest the news, and her look of shock and dismay rattled Ryan's confidence. "You mean you are the owner of North Pole?" she asked. Heather's tone was not congratulatory but confused.

"Pretty much," Ryan confirmed, starting to backpedal a bit. "I own 55% of North Pole, so though I am equal with the board members in process, I have the deciding and authoritative vote for decisions, vision, mission, and even operations. Some owners are very active in companies; some are hands off. . . ."

"So, you own North Pole?" Heather repeated incredulously, cutting Ryan off.

"Yes, I guess I do," Ryan offered sheepishly, looking away to avoid the temptation to offer an angry retort.

Heather sat in silence for a while and felt betrayed. After an awkward few minutes, she shifted the conversation into an interrogation. "If you own North

Pole, does that mean you are resigning from Emerging and moving to Sugar Grove for sure?"

Ryan sensed the shift in her demeanor and immediately became more defensive in posture and position, their old habits of conflict management momentarily resurfacing. "That's the plan, but I am waiting to hear back from Emerging and whether they would allow me to be a remote CEO while owner of another company."

"That seems absurd. Why would they do that?" Heather said with disgust and a mocking laugh, which really bothered Ryan and hit his ego directly.

"I know it, but I do have a strong track record, and the chair of the board seemed open to the idea when we talked this morning. And It gets even more interesting than that," Ryan offered, wanting to gain control of the conversation.

"Go on," Heather encouraged him, but more like a prosecuting attorney than a supportive girlfriend.

Chapter 20

"Today at my brunch meeting with John and the others, they asked me if I would be the president of North Pole." He reported this with pride and a tinge of arrogance, thinking for sure that this would induce celebration from Heather.

Heather narrowed her eyes and stared at Ryan inquisitively. She didn't believe him right away, but his cocky smirk let her know it was true. Now, she was even more angry. "Why would the board want the owner, who already owns the controlling interest, to be the president, running day-to-day operations and having oversight as well?" She didn't let Ryan answer and moved into further disappointment. "And we haven't had a president at North Pole for at least 20 years. Why do we need one? And why haven't they talked to the leadership team about this possibility?" Heather had her arms crossed. Her face was flushed, and she intentionally moved her foot, the one Buford was resting on, letting his snout hit the floor as she glared at Ryan.

Ryan took a condescending tone and fired right back as he snapped his fingers and Buford obediently came to his side. "I can't answer the process questions or the North Pole leadership issues – I'll work on those when I take over – but I know I am more excited about being the president of North Pole than I am of being just the owner. The president is present and working with the people, casting vision, creating new markets, exploring partnership opportunities, expanding the brand, being an advocate for North Pole and Sugar Grove 24/7, just like my grandfather was. It's obvious you are not excited about either of these options, about my being a part of North Pole or maybe even about me at all."

Heather needed to retreat, but she was too angry to back down, feeling now as if she were defending herself and the company from a hostile takeover. "On the one hand, Ryan, it seems like one way or the other, you'll be back in Sugar Grove for good very soon, and that's great." Though that certainly sounded more like a concession than a celebrative response, she continued. "On the other hand, as a Vice President at North Pole, the idea that these major strategic initiatives are in process without my knowledge is disconcerting to say the least, and the fact that my boyfriend, who has ignored the company for the last seven years, has had North Pole handed to him – and then can be installed as president without any due process – is just hard to take." She paused for a moment and Ryan started to respond, but she talked over him and kept going. "And will we even have a CEO anymore? My boyfriend would become my boss, which is not very fun or romantic to imagine. We are both stubborn and proud people, Ryan. Do you think we can handle that kind of work relationship? I don't. I'm sorry. I'm a bit confused and frustrated by all of this." Tears were streaming down Heather's face, but they weren't tears of happiness.

Ryan sat back on his couch, defeated and hurt. He tried to digest her dismay at his amazing news. Of course, she made some valid points, but Ryan had hoped her joy in his return to Sugar Grove would outweigh everything else. It didn't. Ryan was disappointed by her questions and the interrogation and the absence of any excitement and curiosity. He was a little nervous to continue, but he felt he must respond to her last rant. He went the wrong direction with his counter.

"If Josh hadn't come back to town, would you still be confused by the news your boyfriend was about to move back to town to take over his father's company and to be with his girlfriend and son?"

"That's not fair, Ryan," Heather said quickly and strongly. "I didn't invite Josh back, nor did I know anything about his whereabouts. Your father held that information away from everybody." She was really mad now and did feel some guilt about her response. "And no, I don't think Josh's return has anything to do with my feelings about North Pole ownership and the presidency role. If I look at it objectively, I know you will do an amazing job. I just feel like I might have to resign if you come on board. The whole thing will look strange, and people will think every time something good happens with my team that you had something to do with it. I worked really hard to earn that vice presidency, Ryan, and it feels like you just pulled my credibility out from under me."

"Now, who is being absurd?" Ryan challenged and leaned forward. His face was getting red, and his heart rate increased. "I told the board if you had to give up your job that I was refusing the offer. Maybe that's what I need to do then, just turn them down. I can be an owner who lives in the Twin Cities and just visits a couple of times a year." He stood up, wanting to scream or throw something.

Heather stood up also, though neither moved forward. "So, if I resign or threaten to resign you are going to turn down the presidency and stay in the Twin Cities?" Heather said, seriously dejected. "What about us as a couple? What about Henry? You said you wanted to come back to Sugar Grove and be with us."

"I did," Ryan admitted, "and now I am telling you about how that return can happen, but you're telling me that my new positions in North Pole aren't deserved and that they rob you of credibility, so you're going to resign. What kind of president would I be to come in and immediately lose my best VP because of my appointment? I gain a great job, and you lose yours! That would be stupid."

Ryan did not mean to infer that Heather quitting was stupid, but he could tell that is exactly how she took it. She started to leave and go back to the kitchen. She stopped herself and started to speak, but Ryan cut her off to continue.

"And I wasn't even sure you wanted me around anymore anyway. Henry doesn't need me with Josh back in his life, and I don't know how I am going to be able to handle sharing you and Henry with another man. Every time I see you or Henry now, except for this very moment, I have had to share you with him. Is this how it's going to be? Would he be over at the house all the time? I thought you said he was going to only see Josh once a week. Right now, he's seeing him every day. I understand the connection, but can you put yourself in my shoes for a minute? This has been really difficult to mentally absorb. And your questioning my positions with North Pole might hurt even worse than that."

Heather took a step toward Ryan. His passion helped her empathize with him, but Ryan put his hand up to motion Heather not to talk. "I need to go spend some time with Buford and pray." Ryan told Buford to go get his leash and moved to the front door without looking back at Heather.

"Run away, like always," Heather shouted after him as he opened the door and let the screen door bang behind him. She regretted it as soon as she said it, but it was too late.

Ryan stopped on the sidewalk, turned to face her, and started to say something awful, but he thought better of it when Buford excitedly nipped at his hand. Ryan simply shook his head slowly side to side and turned around to find somewhere far away to think.

Heather wanted to run after him and apologize, but she didn't. She went to the window and waited for Ryan and Buford to get into the driveway before she burst into tears and yelled for Becky. Becky had heard the intensity in the conversation and had already been out of the kitchen and in the hallway debating whether to intervene or not. She didn't, but now she was at Heather's side in seconds. The two ladies hugged, and Heather cried some more before they both sat on the couch.

Chapter 20

"I am sick of crying, Becky."

"I know, Honey, but love is messy, and yours is even messier than most right now." Heather and Becky both laughed at that truth as Becky handed Heather some tissues.

"Ryan is so stubborn and proud. I didn't show excitement and enthusiasm for his ownership or presidency of North Pole, so he got defensive and angry and questioned my feelings for Josh, though he didn't say it directly. Then, when I told him I might resign if he became president, he started talking about staying in the Twin Cities again." The more Heather thought about her recap the more frustrated she became. "Argghhhhh, he can make me so mad, Becky."

Becky was quiet for a while and just rubbed Heather's back. How glad Heather was to have a godly woman as a mother figure since her mother was gone. Finally, Becky offered some thoughts.

"Ryan's afraid, Heather. He's afraid of giving up Emerging. He's afraid of moving back to Sugar Grove. He's afraid of not being a good enough father figure to Henry, especially now that Josh is back and doing a great job. He's afraid of disappointing you as a man and a husband. He's afraid of not living up to the standards of his father and his grandfather at North Pole. He's afraid of loving you and losing you."

Heather was reflective and took in the sobering summary. "So instead of working through these fears, he is considering walking away again? He said he would never do that to me or his family again."

"I think that was before Josh returned," Becky countered. "That's thrown everything for a loop."

"Yes, you're right. It has, but isn't my love and Henry's love worth staying for, fighting for?"

"I think you guys just had a fight about that," Becky said with a smile. "And how does Ryan know your feelings haven't changed since Josh came back,

Heather? Have you assured him of your love and commitment to him since Josh is involved again? Even powerful people can become insecure quickly if they aren't 100% sure of the love of their partner. Isn't that what you are feeling right now also?"

Heather thought deeply about the questions. "Yes, it is. I was waiting for Ryan to reassure me of his love, but I know my circumstances and environment have changed, not his. I need to reassure him immediately, but you know your son. I'll have to give him some space and time to process before I run into his arms and declare my commitment again."

"Agreed. Buford and the Lord will take care of him right now. Hopefully, you both can get some time to talk together tonight after Tucker's game and before the service."

"I'll make sure of it, Becky. Thanks for talking with me. You are the only one who knows Ryan better than I do. That helps. And it feels like I have a mother again when I'm around you. That means so much to me."

"I'm so glad, Honey. You can even call me 'Mom' if you want. I'll always be here for you, for both of you, no matter what happens."

Chapter 21

Ryan was furious and set a pace that Buford was not thrilled about keeping. He didn't have time to sniff and mark his path. The tones of Ryan's commands let Buford know it was not a time to push his master's decisions.

"She makes me so mad, Buford! How can she be worried about her career, which isn't going to change at all, when my career is possibly starting over? New town? New role? New responsibilities? Have to prove myself all over again! Where is her risk? I don't understand her insecurity about my position as owner and president. We could be together finally!"

Buford was too focused on their course to offer any verbal response. They were already around the barn, and it was a little slippery. It had snowed a couple of inches throughout the day. Instead of circling the property as they normally did, Ryan led Buford through the timber and onto the main road. They crossed at the four-way, and Ryan found what he was looking for – one of the snow mobile routes the neighbors created every year. Buford was excited by the new adventure and playfully pranced and barked in delight.

It took about a mile, but somewhere between Rural Route 4 and the county state line, Ryan quit complaining and started praying. He asked the Lord for guidance and wisdom, to help him handle Josh's being back in Heather and Henry's life, and to make it really evident to him which way he should go with his career and with his relationships. He thanked the Lord for the incredible opportunities before him, for a great family and his recommitment to them, and for a great father who saw Ryan's future before he did. He apologized to God for his stubborn pride and the neglect in his relationship with both his earthly and heavenly father. He closed his prayer by singing "Amazing Grace."

Buford loved that hymn also and howled in unison with Ryan's deep baritone voice.

Ryan and Buford turned around at the railroad crossing, which was about two miles from his mother's house. Pulling out his phone, Ryan saw it was 2:30. They needed to start back. His family might not be nervous about his safety, but they would be nervous that he wouldn't attend the game. And Heather was right. Ryan did run away from problems he couldn't solve, and he needed to go back and talk with her again. He texted Jennifer and his mother that he was on his way back and should be home by about 3:00. His mother answered, "OK," and Jennifer answered, "Why are you telling me? Tell Heather. Isn't she your girlfriend?" Ryan didn't answer, but she was right; he should be communicating with Heather. He needed to stay assertive and committed in communication and in his belief in their relationship. He didn't want to leave her again. He didn't want to blow a second chance at her love. He pulled up her name and started to text but was interrupted by an incoming call. It was George.

****

Back at South Pole, Josh, Gabe, and Tucker decided to play pool while Henry and Gabby watched the Disney Channel. Jennifer made sure everyone was settled before she found Heather and Becky in the living room. It was obvious Heather had been crying. Heather filled Jennifer in on her fight with Ryan and on Becky's assessment of Ryan's fear. The three women talked about love and the male ego but didn't come to any grand conclusions. After about 20 minutes, Becky checked the time and then headed to the kitchen to make a snack before they left for the game.

Jennifer encouraged Heather to call Ryan out on his passivity, to assure him of her love, and to ask him to lead at the same time. It was not an oxymoron. If Ryan wasn't leading something or someone, he didn't invest in the situation, and that included her. This scared Heather, but she knew she needed to give Ryan time to process the fear and confusion. She didn't want to have to convince him to invest in her and Henry. Ryan seemed more excited about North Pole than he was about their relationship. This was one of her soul fears. Ryan would be so committed and invested in North Pole that she and Henry would be an afterthought. She would rather stay single than be neglected and abandoned all over again. Jennifer understood her fears but encouraged her to give Ryan a chance to be the man he and she both knew he could be.

Furthermore, Jennifer challenged Heather to quit being so dramatic about her job at North Pole. Ryan would not treat her differently because they were a couple – or even if they married. She reminded Heather who Ryan was as a leader. Ryan would be so professional Heather would probably wonder at times if they were even together. This was a benefit of Ryan's personality in the work environment. Why would Heather walk away from her vice presidency because other people talked about their relationship? Who cared what other people thought about her and Ryan and about her success or his success? Heather felt remorse for her defensive rant about North Pole and was inspired by her best friend and Becky to dig deeper into the relationship. Then Jennifer showed Heather the text Ryan just sent and proceeded to read aloud her sassy reply. Both girls giggled but agreed Ryan probably wouldn't text Heather right away, and he didn't.

****

A second call from George on Christmas Eve was surprising, but, like Ryan, George was an obsessive man who liked to handle work things immediately and directly. There was not the familiar greeting, however, when Ryan said hello, so he knew something wasn't right.

Chapter 21

"I sent a quick email to the full board after our talk this morning Ryan, and unfortunately, a majority of the members are not in favor of sharing you with North Pole. "

"OK, I understand," Ryan said calmly, though his head was pounding and his heart raced.

"And because you are already the majority owner of North Pole, and because we know the kind of executive you are, the board feels it will be best for both sides if we part ways sooner than later." George paused in case Ryan wanted to respond, but Ryan was too shocked to offer anything other than silence. George continued, "Unless you decide to relinquish your controlling interest of North Pole, the board authorized me to inform you your tenure with Emerging will be over after the January 5th board meeting. We will, however, give you your full executive commission from the new agreement. You earned that." Again, George was quiet to allow Ryan to speak, but Ryan was too shocked and sad to comment. Finally, George ended the call with, "We would also like you to sell your shares in Emerging as your role as owner of North Pole invokes the no-compete clause. I reviewed all these matters, dates, and times with your contract and with HR, so I know this is valid and reasonable. There will be a nice severance package that you deserve through June. You did amazing work for Emerging, Ryan, and we will miss you. I am really sorry to see you go."

Finally, Ryan responded. "Thanks, George. I understand. And I won't be giving up controlling interest of my family's business, so I guess I will tender my formal resignation next week."

"Thanks," George responded. "If you can have it to me on Monday that would help us all start moving forward. I hope it works out well for you at North Pole."

"Me, too," Ryan concurred. And with that, nearly a decade of dedication, commitment and loyalty was over. *Wow. When you pray earnestly to the Lord you receive immediate answers even if they are not exactly what you expected.* He wandered around the area for a while and allowed Buford to sniff, snort, investigate, and explore as he pondered the termination and the events of the past week. He was definitely hurt by the Emerging board's decision, but he understood their position and wasn't angry. He also was ready for a change and needed some new challenges. Now he knew for sure his career would be with North Pole, so the transition could happen fairly quickly.

Ryan gave Buford a few more minutes and then headed toward home. He contemplated whom to call first with this news. Pulling up Pastor Steve's number, he gave him a call. He decided to wait until he was home to tell everyone else in person. What a Christmas Eve this had been so far, and it was only half over. A mile into his trip back, Ryan recognized the resignation from Emerging was another Christmas setback, but he also recognized his perspective about major life events had changed. "Christmas Eve Obedience," Ryan said out loud to himself and Buford. If he viewed these losses as movements of the Lord and as a result of obeying and following what the Lord had allowed to happen, he could easily find an eternal perspective. If Emerging would have offered a huge raise, more stock options, new staff, new facilities, and more perks, it would have been harder to leave. Now, because of being let go, it allowed Ryan to have immediate closure and to start his transition back home. He was actually finding joy in this startling revelation. Man and dog picked up their pace. If they hustled, they could be home by 3:00 or a little after.

****

Tucker and Gabe left for home around 2:00 to get Tucker's gear and to be at the rink at 2:45. Josh and the kids finished watching Disney at 3:00 when Becky called them upstairs for some snacks before everyone would load up for the game. Jennifer and Heather had enjoyed some tea and conversation, and then went over to the barn to finalize details for the wedding in two days. Heather started to feel some hope and excitement for Ryan's work at North Pole. She also realized she had to learn how to navigate life with a boyfriend and the father of her son at the same time. It would take time to find rhythms and routine that worked and were appropriate. It had only been a few days. Helping Jennifer lifted her mood.

By 3:15, everyone sat around the kitchen counter eating North Pole popcorn, fruit and veggies, and some mini-sandwiches. Jennifer and Heather gathered the coats, snow pants, sweatshirts, gloves, mittens, and boots and brought them near in preparation for departure. They were just finishing up when Ryan walked in the door.

"Hey, did I miss snack time?" Ryan bellowed playfully.

"Yes," Henry shouted.

"We ate it all," Gabby said smugly.

Buford rushed to the kids to see what leftovers might come his way, bread crusts and bits of popcorn as it turned out.

Ryan kept his coat on when he saw the kids' collection in the corner. "Before we head to the game," Ryan said loudly, "I have an announcement to make." Heather and Jennifer looked at each other quickly. "While on my walk with Buford, I received a call from the board chair of Emerging letting me know I've been terminated." Jennifer gasped and Becky said, "Oh my goodness." Heather's jaw dropped. Ryan continued, with a smile on his face. "They are unwilling to share me with North Pole, and I am unwilling not to be owner and President of North Pole. In two weeks, I will pack my bags and move back to Sugar Grove."

The kids didn't understand the big words but understood Ryan was moving back home, and they yelled in delight. Both Henry and Gabby ran to embrace Ryan.

Becky moved closer to Ryan and gave him a hug over the children's embrace and asked if he was OK. "I am doing great, Mom. I'm actually relieved the decision has been made for me. I believe it was an answer from the Lord. I will talk to John and the North Pole board on Monday and make plans for my transition. I might need to live with you for a while until I buy a house."

"Of course," Becky replied.

Jennifer waited to hug him and welcome him back home and then ushered the kids towards the restroom for a bathroom break before they dressed in their winter gear for the game.

Josh moved in next and gave Ryan an enormous bear hug that knocked Ryan back a step. Josh then pulled his head back but did not let go of Ryan. Instead, he grasped him by both shoulders and stared into his eyes. "I am glad you are coming back to Sugar Grove, Ryan. Looks like the Lord had us both return home." It was a profound statement, and both men recognized the depth of the revelation. Josh continued. "I hope we can become good friends. I need some godly men in my life." Josh finally let go of Ryan and stepped back a bit but slid his arm off of his shoulder and grabbed both his wrists, holding them tightly. He disclosed more, "I would be honored if you would be an accountability partner with me. I know you haven't been an addict and I have a sponsor already, but I need a brother to pray with me, to have lunch together once in a while, to help me stay engaged in the Church and in the community."

Ryan was flabbergasted and tried to reconcile the jealousy he had felt two hours ago with the honor he experienced now. He paused, but not too long to be awkward, and then replied, "It would be my privilege, Josh. It looks like we might be suitemates at the South Pole for a while anyway. And for what it's worth, I think you are doing an awesome job reconnecting with Henry. I look forward to doing things with both of you in the future."

This seemed to satisfy Josh, and he quickly turned and glided out of the kitchen. He descended the stairs to the basement to change into warmer clothes. That left only Heather with Ryan. She stepped toward Ryan and Ryan started his apology.

"Heather, I am so sorry for my poor communication and . . .," but before Ryan could say more, Heather moved into his chest and gave him a passionate kiss. Ryan wrapped his arms around her, the confirmation of their relationship they both desperately needed. They finally separated and Ryan said, "I guess that means you're sorry also?" They both laughed.

"It sure does," Heather confirmed.

"Christ Only Exalted," Ryan said softly, looking upward.

"What?" Heather asked innocently.

"Christ Only Exalted," Ryan repeated. "I know you know what that means, but I'll explain why I said it and what it means to me on the way to the game." He kissed her one more time and then pitter-patter boot stomps and snow pants fabric-friction bounded their way.

****

Tucker's team dominated the overmatched opponent 6-1, with Tucker scoring two more goals. The Miller family sat proudly in attendance by gender: Gabe, Ryan, Josh, and Henry in the front row, and Heather, Jennifer, Becky, and Gabby in the second row right behind them, though Gabby spent one period on her dad's lap and one on her uncle's. Everybody waited in the parking lot to congratulate Tucker before they headed to their homes to change for the Christmas Eve service at 8:00. Josh rode with Becky and Ryan. Gabe dropped Heather and Henry off before heading home with his family. They would need a quick turnaround. It was already after 7:00.

****

Pastor Steve's Christmas Eve message was about the context and environment surrounding Bethlehem, Israel, and the Jewish community prior to the birth of Jesus. He talked about our need to anticipate the Lord and His provision even in the midst of silence, challenge, fear, and confusion. Jesus came into the world in humble circumstances. His birth wasn't into royalty; it was into poverty. His applications of practicing obedience even when it doesn't make sense, as Mary did, and to sacrifice even when others will question you, as Joseph did, resonated with the congregation.

Ryan, Becky, and Heather waited to approach Steve in the foyer after he had hugged and encouraged the last of the silent-night worshipers. Josh was in the basement packing his meager belongings and would join them soon. It had been a packed sanctuary with well over 300 people. Gabe and Jennifer had stayed home with Tucker, Gabby, and Henry, who were worn out and needed sleep for the big Christmas celebration the next day.

"You didn't have to preach directly to me so specifically, Pastor," Ryan said with a warm smile and handshake as Josh rejoined the group with a joyful smile.

Steve laughed and gave each of them a big hug, observing the four of them together with a warm smile. "What a blessing the Miller family has been to this church and community, and it looks like the family is expanding." As he turned to Becky, he added, "Your obedience and sacrifice, Becky, allowed me to speak to a full sanctuary at maximum capacity tonight. Our old sanctuary would have held less than half. Thank you!"

"You are so welcome," Becky replied. "Jim believed the Lord asked him to give the funds for this new building. We prayed about it for a month and when we were still at peace and confirmed in our soul, we simply showed up at your office and handed you the check."

"I remember that moment very well," Steve said fondly. "It's not an everyday experience for a pastor."

After a moment of quiet, Ryan interjected, "Well, it is one of those days again today. My mom and I looked over our father's estate and believe the Lord asked us to give another special Christmas gift to the church."

Josh felt he was interrupting a Miller family moment and began to head for the door. "I'll wait for you guys over there," Josh whispered to Becky.

"Nonsense," Becky retorted quietly and grabbed his arm and brought him even closer into the group. "Josh, this gift also directly impacts you and your future." Josh looked startled and waited on Ryan like the others.

Ryan gave Steve an envelope and asked him to open it. Steve obliged and stumbled backwards after he read the amount on the check. It was for two million dollars.

"This check is for the building of the Sugar Grove Restoration Center," Ryan began. "My mom will be the chair of the board, Heather, Jennifer, and I will be the founding board members, and Josh," – Ryan shifted his gaze from Steve to Josh – "you will have the first interview to be our executive director." Becky gave the shocked Josh a big squeeze as Ryan continued. "We want the center to have a strong addictions-recovery component, but that won't be its entire focus. We will work with you and Renee, and whoever else we prayerfully select on this board to bring many restoration opportunities to the community – after-school tutoring, a resale shop, family counseling, leadership development, financial recovery, and whatever else the Lord asks us to provide."

Becky, Heather, and Josh were in tears. Steve knelt down, still in his robe, so taken by the revelation and generosity that he could no longer stand. After a minute, Josh left Becky's arm and pulled the pastor up into his arms for one of his new, powerhouse, suffocating embraces. "We will be able to help so many people, Pastor," Josh said as he kept Steve upright with his vice grip hands and he smiled so broadly and joyfully that Steve began to laugh.

"You are so right, Josh. Why am I so overwhelmed by the Lord's movements? I just taught on the provisions of God when we are waiting for His leading. I believe we just heard from Him loudly and clearly. Let me put this check in the office and then let's go to the sanctuary and have a prayer of blessing over this gift and the Lord's plans for it."

Chapter 22

Christmas day was so fun and peaceful Ryan couldn't believe he had skipped the last seven of them. For what? Pride? Fear? Justified righteousness of his positions? The morning started for him at Heather's. He, Josh, and Buford arrived together at 8:00. Josh would need rides for another week until he received a new driver's license the second week of January and his new truck right after that. Heather made an egg casserole, and Henry basked in the masculine love of both his father and his new favorite uncle. They ate, opened gifts, and sang some Christmas carols and ended with a time of prayer. Buford received a squeaky raccoon doll named Rocky from Henry. When Henry wasn't looking, Ryan used his knife to cut out the squeak box and would ask his mother to sew Rocky back up later that afternoon. They cleaned up a little bit but weren't finished tidying up before they let for the family lunch at South Pole at noon.

****

Becky joined Jennifer's family for their annual Christmas morning. She arrived around 8:00. This would be her first Christmas as a widow, so she was glad to be with family. Jennifer had baked a Christmas cinnamon roll that sent the family into a sugar comatose, though she also provided some sausage and bacon to make sure there was some protein balance. After their presents and clean-up, Gabe announced he was accepted into University of Minnesota's graduate program for education and would begin classes in a few weeks. The family all clapped for him. Then he announced that in April they would put their house on the market, and by June, after school was out, they would move in with Becky at the South Pole. Jennifer had wanted Gabe to talk to the children about the possibility prior to the disclosure, but Gabe was confident in their decision and in their response, so Jennifer conceded. He was right. The kids cheered, and Tucker ran to hug his dad while Gabby jumped onto Becky's lap and started negotiating for her favorite room right next to Becky's.

****

Everyone met back at South Pole at noon but decided not to eat until later in the afternoon. Becky was glad because she had a surprise arranged for the family and ushered everyone down to the basement. After instructing everybody to sit in the theater area, she grabbed the remote, pressed a button, and home videos from Jennifer and Ryan's childhood appeared on the screen. Gabe obviously helped her prepare for the moment because Becky had no idea how to operate any modern technology, and neither Ryan nor Jennifer knew about the videos. Grandpa Joe was there in his Santa suit, and Jim, Ryan, and Jennifer all sported elves' costumes. Immediately Henry and Gabby asked to wear the suits, so Becky pulled them out of the bag she had ready in anticipation. Josh disappeared for a moment and came back out of his room dressed as Santa before they all headed upstairs to open presents.

****

On Sunday before Church, Ryan had breakfast with John and Robert Morrison, and after some soft negotiation, they agreed to the principal terms of his impending contract. After church the Miller family, which now included Heather, Henry, and Josh, ate leftovers at Becky's. They had a peaceful and non-dramatic lunch and then everyone went back to their respective homes. Ryan packed his bags, and on his way out of town, stopped by Heather's for a hug and a kiss and then headed back to the Twin Cities to begin the process of packing, placing his house on the market, and finalizing his paperwork for Emerging. It would be a busy, but hectic week and a busy and chaotic January.

****

Chapter 22

Josh and Becky spent the afternoon taking down Christmas decorations and helping Jennifer with some last-minute decorations for the wedding that started at 4:00. Josh would be a great addition for the family events and Jennifer with his work ethic and willingness to serve. It also gave Gabe a second adult male to carry and move heavy props, tables, chairs, and bales of hay. The fire chief attended the wedding and reception and approached Josh as the party wound down. Josh informed him of his job with the Restoration Center, but that he would still like to be reinstated and drive part-time for the department for free to pay off the money he had stolen from the city during his addiction. The fire chief gladly accepted the offer and would write up a contract and they could finalize the agreement on Monday.

****

On Monday morning, Ryan announced his shocking departure to his entire team at Emerging, provoking a mixture of tears and congratulations. He assured them George and the board would bring an excellent replacement and informed them of the additional agreements with the acquisition company, which would give them an additional bonus, as well. This certainly helped temper the loss. Tammy asked for a private meeting and told Ryan if he were moving to Sugar Grove, so was she. Did North Pole have any work for her? Ryan was thrilled, for the family had already decided to offer her the director role at the new Sugar Grove Restoration Center. She had the perfect complementary personality, temperament, and skillset for Josh as the Executive Director. Recently divorced and without children, Tammy was ready for a fresh start, having no strings attached to the area. A quick video conference with the Center's board, and Tammy was the second hire – and yet another temporary resident at the South Pole "boarding house" during this homecoming season.

Chapter 22

******

When the video call was over, Josh asked a ton of questions about Tammy, and most of them had nothing to do with her competence or career experience. Tammy was a triathlete, an avid skier and hiker, and was as fit and toned as Josh. The girls laughed at the possibility, but Josh was serious. He wanted to know about her faith, her first marriage, and any other details they knew, which wasn't much. He asked Heather for Ryan's number and called his new best friend right away. "Tell me about Tammy!" Josh asked Ryan, without any other introduction.

Ryan understood the intention and didn't pretend to be guarded since Tammy was still in his office. "What do you want to know?" he inquired playfully.

Josh, ever the assertive soul fired off some rapid questions: "Is she single? Would she date a man in recovery? Where does she train? Where is she going to live?"

Ryan laughed and revealed his secret. "Tammy is here with me and heard all your questions. I'll give her my phone, leave the office, and let her answer." Ryan didn't wait for a response and simply handed the dumbfounded Tammy his phone and then quickly exited the room and shut the door quietly behind him. He didn't get his phone back for over an hour.

About the Author

Elliott J. Anderson is Assistant Professor of Psychology and Pastor to Staff and Faculty at Judson University. He is also Pastor of Solid Rock Free Will Baptist Church in Elgin. Elliott is partner of CORE13 LLC, a construction and painting company and counsels in private practice. He is a regularly featured guest as a psychotherapist on Dr. Karin, Love and Life Media (loveandlifemedia.com). He has written articles for Leadership, Christianity Today, Today's Christian Living, Adoptive Families, and College Faith 2. Elliott serves on the Board of Engage Africa (engageafrica.com) and Nationwide Chaplain Services (emergencyresponsechaplainservices.org) and is a consultant for Constant Organization Development (constantod.com).

Elliott's previous books are *It's About Time*, Clifton Hills Press 2021, *Simon Says, Principles and Perspectives from Dr. Simon V. Anderson*, Clifton Hills Press 2020, and *Answers in Abundance, A Miraculous Adoption Journey As Told From A Father's Heart*, Morgan James Publishing 2007. Look for *Negotiating the Bonds of Love: Understanding Attachment and Intimacy in Marriage* in 2022.

For more information, insights, or requests, for counseling please contact Elliott at elliott.anderson@judsonu.edu. You can also follow him on Instagram @pastorelliottanderson for up-to-date information about future publications, speaking, and more.

Made in the USA
Monee, IL
30 December 2021

86619595R00233